FORSAKEN

FORSAKEN

Kelley Armstrong

ILLUSTRATIONS BY XAVIÈRE DAUMARIE

SUBTERRANEAN PRESS 2015

First Edition

ISBN
978-1-59606-691-5

Subterranean Press
PO Box 190106
Burton, MI 48519

subterraneanpress.com

One

THE ONLY THING worse than being summoned to a pointless meeting? Being summoned three thousand miles to a pointless meeting when you're about to embark on your annual family vacation.

Clay and the twins were in a lovely log cabin in Vermont. And me? I was sweating in a tiny oven of a meeting room somewhere in London. For absolutely no goddamned reason except that the British Alpha insisted I come, and I was trying to claw my way out of the hole I'd fallen into three years ago when I became Alpha of the American Pack.

"As long as we have your assurances that he'll behave himself, he's welcome in the States," I said. "We won't bother him."

"I should hope not, considering he's my son." That was Hollis John Parker, British Alpha, Lord something-or-other. I could never remember his title. Nick called him Lord Asshole. Not exactly poetic, but apt.

"The fact that he's your son doesn't mean he isn't..." I struggled for a polite way to phrase it. "Young and spirited. I understand the French Pack kicked him out of Paris for changing into a wolf in the catacombs?"

"He was a child then."

"It was six months ago."

"He's eighteen now."

And so it went. Parker's son had decided to go to Berkeley, and he'd summoned me to England to discuss the transfer, which I'd thought proved he was actually taking me seriously as Alpha, but as it turned out, he'd ordered me there because he seemed to be under the impression America was still a British colony.

He didn't care to convince me his son could handle life abroad without another "Paris incident." He expected my Pack to act as bodyguards for the boy. For me to order one of my guys to move across the country to do it.

Two hours later, I was striding down a London street with Nick beside me. When my phone rang, I yanked it out of my pocket so fast it slid from my fingers. Nick managed to grab it before it hit the pavement.

He started to hand it back, still ringing. Then he glanced at the screen and made a face. "Private caller. You want me to—"

"Please."

He answered with a, "Hello?" Then another one.

"Hang up," I said. "Bad enough I still get telemarketers when I'm on the do-not-call list. Worse when I get charged international rates for them."

As soon as I took the phone, it rang again, Private Caller flashing on the screen.

"Okay," I muttered. "Someone is about to get the brunt of my very bad day." I answered with a snarled, "What?"

"It's six o'clock," said a sing-song voice. "Do you know where your puppy is?"

Click. I pulled the phone from my ear and stared at it. Then I laughed.

"Not a telemarketer, I take it?" Nick said.

"No, a kid making a prank call. My first in about thirty years, I think."

"What'd he ask?"

"If I know where my puppy is."

Now Nick laughed. "Okay. Well, I think we can declare the art of phone pranks has officially died out. That makes no sense."

"Unless I had a puppy."

"Do you want a puppy?"

"No, but I'll take a drink."

He smiled. "I have a feeling that'll cheer you up better than a puppy. And that looks like a pub right there. Shall we?"

"Please."

*

ALPHA OF THE American Pack. The only female werewolf in the world, ascending to arguably the highest position in our world. Sounds impressive. The truth? It's like getting elected town sheriff because no one else wants the damn job. And like taking it—not because you've always dreamed of being sheriff—but because, well, someone has to.

I like being Alpha. There are days—hell, even weeks sometimes—where I feel like I've found my place. Like I'm blessed with a damned-near perfect life. I'm forty-three, fit and healthy. I'm crazy about my mate, even when he *drives* me crazy. Same goes for my eight-year-old twins. I have great friends and an incredible Pack. And, of course...*Alpha*.

I can say there were no other contenders, but the others would argue that they didn't want the job because they knew it was mine, that Jeremy had been grooming me since I got my shit together and recommitted to the Pack thirteen years ago. The only other possibility had been Clay, who really didn't want the position.

While he'd never admit it, I think Clay removed himself from the running so Jeremy didn't have to make a very tough choice. Clay is perfect twentieth-century Alpha material. He's the best fighter in the country—remorseless and relentless. Also brilliant. But that doesn't fly in the twenty-first century, when Alphahood is more about politics than pugilism. Jeremy says he'd have given me the position anyway, but I'm not sure he could have done that to his foster son. I suspect it would have been a joint ascension—an Alpha pair, like in a real wolf pack.

Sometimes I wish he'd actually done that. Made us both Alpha. Because to most of the world, I'm a figurehead, placed in a false position of power to appease those werewolves who'd freak out if "that American psycho" got the job. We've spent three years unsuccessfully trying to convince the world Clay isn't the real Alpha, and the situation has gone from damned annoying to downright dangerous.

We've made enemies of the Australian Pack, which is a lot scarier than one might expect. It started by us defending our own young Australian member—whose only crime seemed to be his very existence—and had somehow escalated into war-mongering. The Australians wanted our territory, and they used me to gain allies, saying that even pretending to have a woman in charge proved the American Pack was weak.

The Australians have amassed an army of allies from smaller Packs, mostly third-world and developing countries who'd love a piece of the American dream. On our side, we had the Russian Pack. That's it. Other Packs—French, German, Italian—support us in theory, but in practice, if we're invaded, their troops are staying home and cheering us on from the sidelines.

The biggest problem is the Brits. They're a big Pack and they're spoiling for a fight, and they haven't yet decided whose side they'd take. Parker has said there is a way to secure his help. Just let him deal with the real Alpha: Clay. And if my leadership isn't a ruse, then I should *make* Clay the Alpha and step the hell down. I don't dare tell him what I think of that suggestion, so all I can do is show up here without Clay in tow and try to prove I'm the real deal. So far, I'm failing miserably. ⌒

Two

HE NEXT AFTERNOON, I was back in a meeting with Parker and struggling to hold my temper.

"I want Marsten," Parker said. "Antonio Sorrentino has a better reputation as a fighter, but he's old." Beside me, Nick stiffened at the insult to his father. Parker smirked. Lord Asshole indeed.

"Karl Marsten has a wife and three-year-old daughter. He's not moving to California for the school year."

"Are you saying you can't make him? That you would allow a Pack member to claim *family responsibilities* and ignore a direct order?"

That barb hit home. Of all my Pack, Marsten was the only one not completely under my control. I can boss him around better than Jeremy could, but if I was to *order* him to California for eight months? I'd fail.

"I could send Morgan Walsh for a month, to help Kevin get settled in."

"Who?" Parker's face screwed up. "Oh, yes. The *Canadian.*" He added a derisive twist to the word, knowing full well where my own passport came from. "He's a nobody. I want someone with a reputation."

"Reese, then."

Parker sputtered. "Send my son to school with the Aussie brat at the center of this whole crisis? Not unless I want him to major in rape."

I struggled to keep my tone steady. "Reese was seduced by the Alpha's mate when they were in college together, because she wanted to secure her position by handing over Reese's parents. Which she did. And the Australian Pack slaughtered them."

"So Reese says. You believe him because he's a confused young wolf and you're a mother. It makes you susceptible."

"Excuse me? If I had absolutely any doubt—"

Nick's hand tightened on my leg. I had to calm down, and what made that even harder was knowing that if Clay was here, he'd go for Parker's throat—figuratively and perhaps even literally. And Parker would respect him for that. If Clay snarled and raged, he was a proper werewolf. If I did, I was a hysterical woman.

"You can have Morgan or Reese for two months," I said. "Or you can have Karl for one. Your choice."

"Karl for the entire school year. August to May." He smiled, showing his teeth. "Of course, he'll get the holidays off, to visit his family."

"If he goes for one month, his family will go with him."

Nick murmured, "I'll do it. Two months."

I looked over. He nodded.

"All right," I said. "Nick for two months."

Kevin—sitting beside his father—snickered. "The omega? I'd rather take the retard."

Nick shot to his feet, his face hard. "Don't you—"

"—call you the omega?"

"I don't give a damn what you call me, boy. But you don't use that other word for *anyone*. Presuming you're talking about Noah, I don't know what you've heard, but he's in college with an IQ of a hundred and ten, which I'm going to guess is about twenty points higher than yours."

"Enough," I said. "Noah has school, so he's not an option. Nick is, and considering he sent Malcolm Danvers running, I don't think you really want to call him the omega. Let's cut through the insults and—"

"About Malcolm Danvers," Parker said. "He's still on the run, I hear."

"We're—"

"On the run for three years now, since he escaped Nast custody. Two years since Nicholas here found him."

I tried not to growl. Parker knew exactly what was going on with Malcolm, because I'd kept him in the loop. When Nick and Vanessa tracked down Malcolm, she'd implanted a tracking device. But just because we could find him didn't mean we could catch him, not without losing some of my Pack. Malcolm had high-tailed it to Bulgaria, where the local Pack refused to extradite him.

For over a hundred damned years, the American Pack had had little to no contact with our international brethren. Now I seem to spend half my time putting out cross-border fires.

"We're handling Malcolm," I said to Parker.

"Not very well."

True, and if you'd get off your ass and pull your weight with the Bulgarians, maybe we could get the psychotic bastard extradited.

"Back to the point, again," I said. "I'm offering—"

My cell started playing *Bad Moon Rising*. Clay's tone. Our daughter, Kate, had set it up. She thought it was hilarious. The British Pack stared like I'd broken out in song myself.

"Interesting choice," Parker said.

"My daughter's," I murmured, taking the phone. I looked at the accompanying picture. Clay with Kate—her choice again.

"It's Clay," Nick said. "And he wouldn't interrupt unless it was urgent Pack business."

Thank you. "Right," I said. "Sorry, but I need to grab this."

I took the phone and hurried into the hall. I answered just as it was about to go to voice mail.

"Hey," I said. "What's—"

"Where are you?"

I paused. The voice on the other end wasn't my mate's Louisiana drawl, but a little girl's, pitched high with annoyance.

"Kate?" I said, then lowered my voice quickly, before anyone heard me talking to my kid. "Is something wrong?"

"Yes. We're on vacation. Our one family vacation a year. And you're not here. You're on business."

I squeezed my eyes shut. *Not now, Kate. Damn it, not now.*

Kate has always been very vocal in her objections to either Clay or me traveling. I could point out that ninety percent of our lives are spent at Stonehaven, where the kids have only to shout to find us. Jeremy says that's the problem—they're so accustomed to having us close that they get out of sorts when we aren't. As they've gotten older, though, Kate's complaints have softened. She understands why we leave, and she still doesn't like it, but she's more likely to tease and cajole than actually complain. Until now. My not-quite-nine-year-old daughter had apparently hit adolescent mood swings early.

"When are you coming home?" she demanded.

"Watch your tone. If this meeting wasn't urgent—"

"It's one week a year. One damned week—"

"Kate!"

She barreled on. "—and you can't even be bothered showing up."

"I will be home tomorrow," I said, through gritted teeth. "Your father has my flight information. And you and I are going to have a talk—"

"Hard to do when you're not here. You won't be on that plane. You never—"

"I have never, ever missed a family vacation or any other important event—"

Kate let out a howl that made me jump. The line crackled. Another voice sounded in the background. Logan, who seemed to have wrested the phone from his sister. Then Clay's pounding footsteps and, "What the hell—?"

"She called Mom to whine," Logan said.

A commotion in the background as Clay apparently trotted Kate off. Another crackle on the line, then, "Hey, Mom."

I rubbed my face hard and forced a smile. "Hey, baby."

"Sorry about that. She's being a brat, which is nothing new these days. Hormones."

"She's too young for that."

"Then she has no excuse, does she?"

I laughed and leaned against the wall. My kids. Neither is your typical prepubescent, but they've never been your typical anything. Having werewolves for parents pretty much guarantees that, but it's their upbringing, too. In a

Pack—wolf or werewolf—children are cherished and adored, but never treated like babies. It doesn't help that despite all my efforts to socialize them they've never shown much interest in kids their own age. They have school chums, but mostly to humor me. They're content with their Pack and with each other.

Kate has always been my wild child. Fiercely intelligent and prone to hobbies that involve noise and activity, like music and sports. People joke she's her father's daughter, but I see as much of him in Logan, my quiet, brilliant boy.

"She shouldn't have called," he said. "Dad's giving her proper hell now."

"I can hear that."

For most of their lives, my children had never heard their father raise his voice. To others, yes, but with them, he was a damned-near perfect parent. Better than me at keeping his temper. Yet in the last few months, as Kate's behavior escalated and our bafflement grew, she'd begun getting the sharp side of his tongue, and though it hadn't escalated to shouting matches, it occasionally got close.

"She'll survive," Logan said, as if reading my mind. "She deserves it, because she's being a total brat. Even I can't get through to her. Whatever she said to you, she doesn't mean it. You know that."

"I do. I'm trying to get there as fast as I—"

"You don't need to convince me, Mom. I know you are. *She* knows you are. Here's Dad. I'll go speak to her and give her crap."

I chuckled as he handed the phone over. Logan and Clay exchanged a few murmured words. Then the sound of a door shutting and Clay came on.

"I'm sorry, darling. Guess I have to keep my phone in my pocket."

"I keep telling myself it's a phase, but she's getting worse, and if this is a sign of what we're going to endure for the next five years—"

"Don't even say that. Please."

"I shouldn't let her goad me."

"You usually don't, but I suspect you're getting plenty of goading from Lord Asshole over there. Maybe we can kill two birds with one stone. Reschedule the family vacation. I'll drop the kids off at home with Jeremy and come out there, stand behind you and glower over my ruined vacation. Shut him up and teach Kate that Pack business comes first."

"Which punishes Logan, too, when he's had to put up with his sister's shit as much as we have."

"Yeah..."

"It also gives Parker ammo. Not only do I need to call in my mate for backup, but I'm cranky because I missed out on time with my kids. Typical woman. Once they have kids, you can't rely on them anymore."

"I said *I'd* be the one cranky about missing the family time."

"They'll think you're just upset because you had to 'baby-sit' our kids for a few days while your mate gallivanted off to London. You and I can say the exact same thing, and some-how—" I bit the words off. "God, I'm tired of listening to myself whine."

"*Bitch*, not whine. Justifiable bitching."

"It feels like whining. I wish— Hell, you know what I want? You to drop Kate off with Jeremy and bring Logan to London. Screw this meeting. We'll take Logan to the British Museum and let him explore while we hole up in the nearest hotel and work very hard on helping me forget this crap."

He chuckled. "If I thought you were serious, I'd plunk Kate on a plane to Jeremy, and put Logan and myself on the next one to London." He sobered. "I'm serious, too...though not about sending Kate alone, as tempting as that would be. You say the word and we're there. Tell Lord Asshole he has until tonight to wrap up or you're gone."

I transferred the phone to my other ear.

"Elena?"

"I'm thinking. Shit. I know I shouldn't..."

"Yeah, you should. Not that I'm giving you advice on how to do your job, because that would be wrong..."

I smiled. Technically no one advised the Alpha, except the previous one, but Clay knew full well that I'd never want him to keep his thoughts to himself. It's not as if he could anyway. Physically impossible.

"If you want to call Jer, go ahead," he said. "But we both know what he'd do. Stay and wear them down. Quietly bend them to his will. Me? Hell, I'd have refused to go. If I had to, I'd have stormed out the minute Parker started pulling his shit, which is why I'm not Alpha. But Jeremy's way isn't yours and neither is mine. You've got to do it your way."

"I know. You're right, though. I'm giving him a deadline and then I'm walking away. Tell Kate I'll be on that plane and at the cabin tomorrow morning. Guaranteed. If she still complains, then we go with option two, which is dropping her off at home and you two joining me in London. We need to crack down on her more."

"Yeah, no more excuses. It's been going on too long."

Nick leaned around the corner. I motioned that I'd be right there and signed off. ⌒

Three

I GAVE PARKER THE deadline. He ignored it. When we broke for dinner, I informed him that I had plane tickets for that night.

"Change them," he said, and walked out.

I left through the other door, moving fast, my expression as neutral as I could make it as Nick kept pace beside me.

"Elena?" someone called. When I didn't slow, footsteps pounded closer. "Ms. Danvers? Er, no, it's Michaels, right? You kept your name."

I turned. It was Parker's cousin, Harris Charles Parker. Also Lord something-or-other, but not as deserving of Nick's alternate moniker.

"Ms. Michaels?" he said as he slowed behind us.

I managed a smile. "Either Michaels or Danvers is fine, but Elena's even better. Sorry. Long day."

"And my cousin is an ass, which really doesn't help."

Nick snorted at that. When I didn't respond, Harris made a face. "Sorry. He's still Alpha. I shouldn't say that. But he's only been Alpha for three years. He's been my cousin—and an asshole—for almost fifty. Can I...?" He motioned, asking if he could walk with us.

I nodded, and we continued onto the street.

When we got outside, Harris said, "You're familiar with our ascension issues, I presume? Though you were busy with your own at the time, which went a lot smoother." A nervous smile my way. Trying to be friendly and knowing that, after Parker's dismissal, it was a tough sell.

"I know there was another contender, I said. "Hollis's current beta, Shane Atherton. They seem to have worked it out, though. It was a bloodless ascension, right?"

"Oh, yes. None of that old battle to the death nonsense. We're a little more civilized than that. It's just, well, it was a heated race, bloodless or not. Hollis won by one vote and—" He cleared his throat and glanced around. "We discovered voting irregularities earlier this year."

"Ah."

"That's not unusual with these things, but Hollis... Many of us are concerned about how he's treating you."

"Then you should take that up with him."

As pissed off as I was with Hollis Parker, no way in hell was I saying anything that undermined his authority. An Alpha doesn't do that. However, an Alpha does have options. I gave Nick a look.

"Harris," Nick said. "Elena's got a long flight ahead of her, and she needs to pack and eat, and say goodnight to her kids. How about you and I grab a pint?"

"Hmm?" Harris said. Then, "Oh, of course. Yes. That's fine. My apologies, Ms....Elena. We'll walk you back to your hotel. There's a pub right downstairs."

*

I LET NICK walk me up to my hotel room. Once he was gone, I scooted down the stairwell and out the rear door to find food. As an Alpha off my territory, I shouldn't be walking around unaccompanied. That's the official reason Nick is with me, though the real reason is companionship.

An Alpha always travels with a bodyguard, usually the beta. I wasn't rebelling against that. It's just that while that may be the custom for Alphas, in my case, I worry that it looks like an issue of gender. As if, being a female Alpha, I'm nervous off my territory. Or, worse, that my Pack insists on dogging my steps so no foreign werewolf decides he'd like a shot at the only female of his kind.

That isn't paranoia. I've heard the whispers and snickers about how Clay never leaves my side. At least, unlike Jeremy when he was Alpha, I can go into the bathroom without Clay as escort. No one ever said a word about Clay sticking so close to Jeremy.

I shouldn't let it bother me. It still does. So if I was hungry, I could handle getting food on my own.

I made it exactly one block from the hotel before cursing my mini-rebellion. I was being followed. It wasn't a scent or a sound or a sight that alerted me, but a sixth-sense feeling of a gaze locked on me for longer than it should be.

The chance of spotting my pursuer was next to none. I was on a London street at Friday rush hour. Workers hurried every which way, eager to start their weekend. I took a deep breath. That was more likely to work—even with the overwhelming smells and stenches of a busy city street, my nose was attuned to the faint, musky scent of a werewolf. When I didn't catch that, I considered my options, and that's when I really cursed myself out.

I wasn't in physical danger. I can hold my own against any werewolf. Multiple attackers would be a problem, but that wasn't going to happen on a busy, sunlit street. No, the problem was that no matter what I did next, it could reflect badly on me and, by extension, my Pack. Especially if my pursuer was one of Parker's wolves.

If I headed back without dinner, I looked like a little girl who thinks she's tough but flees at the first sign of danger. Ignore it, and I seemed oblivious to the threat. Go after my pursuer, and I had something to prove.

Damn it, why do I get myself into these situations?

Easy. Because I *do* have something to prove. After twenty years as a vital member of the Pack, with my gender there a non-issue, it had become an issue. I felt like the first female CEO, trying to prove she can do her job while the vultures circle, waiting to snatch her company out from under her.

I sent a text to Nick. *I'm an idiot.*

He replied immediately. *What'd you do?*

Got hungry. Picked up a tail.

Ah. Where are you?

I gave him the street corner.

On my way.

I surveyed the passing streams of people. After sixty seconds, I spotted my pursuer. A man stood with his back to me, watching my reflection through a shop window. Average height, broad shoulders, dark hair. Dressed in jeans and a snug shirt that showed off generous biceps and a well-muscled back. Physically fit. Typical for a werewolf. Our metabolisms run fast and our energy level runs high, meaning it would take concentrated effort—and possibly physical injury—for us to stay sedentary.

It wasn't physical fitness or restlessness that tipped me off, though. In fact, the guy was standing absolutely still. Unnaturally still. A hunter honed in on his prey. His stance gave it away, too. Werewolves are stronger than humans. We live longer. We age slower. We have enhanced reflexes, hearing, smell and night vision. That can lead to a certain... Let's call it what it is. A sense of superiority. The lion at the waterhole. This particular lion was completely focused on me, no self-consciousness or nervousness, not a thought for anyone around him.

Got him, I texted to Nick.

Half a block to go.

Slow down. Heading left. Alley. Follow at distance.

OK.

I took another look at the presumed werewolf. As I did, my gut said, "I know him." Something about his stance or the way he held himself, but it was no more than that, because he had his back squarely to me. Without a face—or a scent— he could be a mutt I'd met five years ago or one of the British Pack wolves. Most likely the latter.

There was no way to get a better look without also letting him know he'd been spotted. So I crossed the road at the light with everyone else and then stood on the other corner and pretended to be looking for a shop sign, checking my raised phone as if consulting a map or compass. Then, with a nod, I did an about-face and marched into an alley.

It was not a particularly dark or deserted alley. It was even clean. But it still proved a little too tempting to my pursuer, and I was about halfway down it when I heard a footfall behind me. A light footfall, one that would have made no noise if it hadn't landed on a stray piece of gravel, stone scraping against the pavement. He might still be close enough to the mouth of the alley to dart out of sight if I turned, so I continued walking.

My phone vibrated with a text from Nick. *Knock, knock. Five sec.*

I slowed to give Nick time to fall in behind and block the alley. I'd gone six steps when a whispered, "Damn," had me turning to see Nick at the other end. He lifted his hands, an apologetic, *I don't know what happened.* There was no one between us.

"I didn't see anyone come out," he said as I headed back to him.

"It's my fault. I heard him and slowed before you texted. He must have gotten spooked and backed out. We'll—"

My phone buzzed. Private Caller. I answered with an annoyed, "Hello?"

"It's six o'clock," a young boy's voice said. "Do you know where your puppy is?"

"Actually, I do. But thanks for checking."

He hung up. I pocketed my phone.

"Your prank caller?" Nick asked.

"Yes. If he does it again, I might be tempted to give him better lines." I looked along the alley and sighed. "My week just keeps getting better. Can you stand watch while I give it the sniff test?"

We walked to the mouth of the alley. Nick leaned against the wall, hands in his pockets, feigning nonchalance while his gaze scanned the passing crowds. I dropped a coin on the ground and crouched to pick it up. I hadn't even gotten within a foot of the pavement before I cursed and straightened.

"Scent blocker," I said.

Nick rolled his eyes. "Figures."

There are commercial sprays and soaps to help hunters eliminate their scent. They aren't magic. Clay and I went after a mutt a few years ago who I swear bathed in a tub of the stuff, which made him easier to track than if he hadn't. Another time a mutt used it to disguise the fact he'd come sneaking around our cabin when Clay and I were having a date weekend. The smell of the scent blocker wouldn't have given him away—we could presume it was an actual hunter—but in a forest environment, it hadn't done enough to block his underlying werewolf scent. In the city, though, I couldn't thread out my stalker's scent from both the blocker and the dense layer of human scents.

"I get the feeling I know him," I said.

"Probably one of Lord Asshole's boys."

"One of whom is sitting back at the pub, wondering what's taking you so long in the bathroom."

"It's the food."

I laughed under my breath and looked out at the busy sidewalk.

"Do you want to track him?" Nick asked.

I shook my head. "Let's get you back to the pub."

Four

*E*IGHT O'CLOCK THE next morning. I was sitting at the Sorrentino residence, an hour north of New York City, taking a break before the five-hour drive to our rented cabin in Vermont. Our outbound plane had been held on the tarmac for over an hour, costing me my connection to Burlington. I'd called Clay as soon as I arrived.

Yesterday, I'd said I'd take a cab from the Burlington airport to the cabin, and he'd agreed, but that was just a game. He tells the kids that I think I'm taking a cab, and then he shuttles them off to the airport to surprise me. Which will work for about four more years, before the twins hit puberty and really don't want to get up early to meet Mom at the airport. I was almost a little relieved to scuttle his plan this time, because I had the feeling Kate would have given him grief, and I'd have shown up at the arrivals gate to find one cranky daughter, one pissed-off husband and one innocent son anxiously trying to calm the rough waters.

When I missed my flight, I decided to drive. Since the Sorrentino estate was on the way, Nick drove me that far, where I'd borrow one of their cars. Now I was relaxing in a recliner talking to Reese. Morgan slipped in, wordlessly handing me a coffee before disappearing deeper into the house. Everyone was home, but they'd all made themselves scarce with one excuse or another, giving me time with Reese before I left.

The current international crisis was, of course, not Reese's fault. He was simply the excuse. He knew that. He's a bright kid. Okay, at twenty-five, he's not really a kid anymore—he's graduated with his MBA and works for Antonio's company. But he's smart and he's also…I wouldn't say sensitive, but he's always been worried about how much he might be imposing on the Pack.

Even before this began, it took years for him to accept the Sorrentino home as his. Sometimes I wonder if the MBA was something he actually wanted or he just got it so he could pull his weight in the family business.

When the crisis first began, Reese had packed his bags and we'd had to track him down, drag him back and put him in the cage at Stonehaven for a week. Which sounds cruel, but that's the language werewolves understand best. *You're*

*important to us and, by God, we're going to keep you safe if we
need to lock you in the basement to do it.*

I wasn't here to remind Reese that this wasn't his fault. But
of course that was implied as we sat and talked about nothing
important, me saying to him, in my way, that however angry I
was at Harris's behavior, it had nothing to do with him.

"Are you seeing Madison this weekend?" I asked as I
sipped my coffee.

"Yes," he said cautiously. "We're still friends."

"Well, I should hope so or I'm more out of the loop than
I thought. I was asking because I need to reschedule my interview with her for next weekend, and I'm hoping you can
convey the message."

"Uh, sure. Right. I'll tell her."

He settled back with obvious relief that I hadn't been
prying in hopes that Reese and Maddie had graduated to
more than friends. Of course I hoped for that. I was pretty
sure Maddie did, too, but she'd accepted friendship. It'd been
almost two years since the Australian Pack sent Maddie's
father, Charlie, on a bounty hunt for Reese, and Maddie had
taken the job instead. She'd discovered that the Australian
Pack's story about Reese was a crock of bullshit.

Eventually she'd take asylum here with Charlie. Her
father had applied for Pack membership, and Maddie had too,
which was a little unusual, considering she wasn't a werewolf.

But my daughter would always be a Pack member—whether she Changed or not—so could I deny membership to a young woman with the blood and the willingness to follow Pack rules and pull her weight? If I didn't let her in, did that make me a hypocrite? If I did, did that open up the Pack too far, risk further damaging our international reputation? It was a thorny situation, one I was still puzzling through. Madison knew that, but we were proceeding with the interview process while I did.

"I'm rescheduling my plans with Maddie, too," Reese said. "I'm driving you up to Vermont."

"What? No. I—"

"You're exhausted and that's no way to start a vacation. I'll drive."

"It's five hours away."

"Exactly. Plenty of time for you to sleep. I have it all worked out. We'll get there by early afternoon. I'll take the kids hiking for a couple of hours while you and Clay have some private time together, then I'll make you guys dinner and be gone by nightfall. Sound good?"

It did. It really did. I could use the rest—and the company—on the long drive. I could definitely use some private time with Clay. And Reese was an excellent cook. Plus the kids adored him, and his visit might even be enough to shake Kate out of her bad mood.

Above all, this wasn't really about me. It was about Reese, desperate to make amends for any role he played, however inadvertently, in this crisis. If I turned down his offer, I robbed him of that chance.

"If you're sure," I said.

He smiled. "Give me five minutes to get ready."

He left. Noah came in, obviously wanting to ask something. My phone buzzed with a number I didn't recognize. I lifted a finger, telling Noah to hold on, and answered tentatively.

"Hey, Momma."

I jerked upright. "Logan? Where are you calling from?"

"Um…the cabin? There's a phone? You know, one of those old-fashioned ones that comes with the house."

I relaxed and muttered, "Smart ass," under my breath. He heard it, of course, and laughed softly, saying, "Long night?"

"Very long. So your dad told you I'm driving up."

"He did. How was your flight?" He prattled on for another thirty seconds, asking about turbulence and the meal service and Nick, barely giving me time to answer, and the more he talked, the tighter I gripped the phone. My son does not prattle. Or he only did under certain circumstances, the same ones that added an uncharacteristically jaunty note to his tone and had him calling me "Momma" like he did when he was little.

"What's wrong?" I said.

37

Silence. Another thing my son doesn't do? Lie. It's not so much an ethical choice as having learned at a very young age that he's horrible at it.

"Something's wrong," I said slowly, struggling to keep my tone even. "As much as I love hearing from you, baby, I know you're not calling to chat."

He inhaled. Then, "I'm going to…I'm going to tell you something, and I need you to just hear me out, all right? Let me finish before you say anything. Okay?"

I've said my son reminds me of his dad, but those lines were straight from Mom's script, normally used when preparing to give bad news to his father.

I clutched the phone so tight my fingers ached. Noah looked alarmed and backed out of the room. The faint thump of footfalls followed.

"Logan," I said. "Tell me what happened."

"It's Kate. She's…" He cleared his throat. "She's playing some kind of game. Nothing to worry about. Dad has everything under control, and it'll all be fine when you get here, but just in case you try calling him before he fixes it, I wanted you to know so he wouldn't need to tell you, because he's a little freaked out and—"

"What happened?"

"She took off." He rushed on before I could say anything. "No one snatched her. There are no other scents in the house. She snuck out before we got up, and now she's hiding in the forest or something stupid like that. Kids do it all the time, Mom. Regular kids. I hear them talk about it at school, taking off to freak out their parents, and I think it's really, really dumb, and normally Kate would too, especially since she knows how you guys worry about us, but with the way she's been, doing something stupid and thoughtless is just what you have to expect and—"

"K-Kate's gone?"

At a noise behind me, I glanced over to see that Antonio and Nick had come into the room. Noah stood anxiously beside them.

"No, Mom," Logan spoke slowly, as if I was eighty-nine and going a bit dotty. "She's taken off. Temporarily. She's being a brat, and I just don't want you talking to Dad because he's already freaked out enough, and it's not his fault—"

"I would *never* blame your father—"

"But he's blaming himself, right? And if he has to tell you he lost her—which he didn't—" Logan inhaled sharply. "If anyone's at fault here, it's me. She got into it with Dad last night, and I gave her crap for that. We had a big fight. She came to my room in the middle of the night and wanted to talk, and I ignored her."

"If Kate took off, then it's no one's fault but her own."

"Right. Exactly." A pause. "Maybe I shouldn't have called."

I squeezed my eyes shut. I needed to get past the panic, to reassure him. God, he was *eight*, he shouldn't *have* to call, shouldn't have to be the one calming *me*, reassuring *me*.

Kate.

Oh God, Kate.

"Mom?"

I took a deep breath. "Sorry, baby. No, you were absolutely right to call. I'll…" I floundered, words drying up as the panic surged. *I'll do what? I'm three hundred miles away and Kate's—* Another deep breath. "I'll be there in a few hours, and I'm sure you'll have her by then."

"We will. Dad's tracking her now. No one came in and grabbed her. No one was lurking in the woods to take her. This isn't werewolf stuff. It's normal kid stuff. Okay?"

"I know." I squeezed my eyes shut and pulled myself together. "You're in the cabin, right?"

"Right."

"Grab something to eat before you go. Make sure you eat and make sure you take something for your dad. He probably won't want it, but if he starts getting cranky, feed it to him."

A soft laugh. "Okay."

"You don't need to tell him you called me if you'd rather not, but it will help if you do. Just say that I know what's happened, and I completely agree she's just taken off, and if he wants to call me, he can, but I'm sure she's fine and when he finds her—"

"—take her back to Stonehaven and lock her in the cage?"

I couldn't help laughing. "No."

"It might help."

"I think we can find normal punishments for normal bad behavior. Just tell him to keep an eye on her. And not to let her eat until I'm there."

"Ouch. That'll teach her."

I smiled. "It might." I signed off and closed my eyes again.

"He's right," a voice said quietly.

I opened my eyes to see Antonio crouching in front of me, hands laced over his knees. "Logan's right. Kids take off. I remember someone"—a look Nick's way—"did it a couple of times before his grandfather really did lock him in our cage for the weekend."

"Don't remind me," Nick said with a shudder.

Antonio smiled. "I still don't know what actually was the bigger hardship, though. The cage or the fact it cost you a weekend with friends." He looked back at me. "Dominic knew we can't have our kids taking off in a snit. It's not safe. If someone wants to get at us? Just go after our children. Can't hurt us worse than that. Which does not mean I'd ever suggest putting Katie in the cage. But normal behavior or not, it's a serious offense. As Logan says, though, no one was lurking outside and snatched her. No one would have known she was there. Clay will find her, and *you* will find a way to impress upon her the severity of her actions." He squeezed my knee. "And that's your task. Don't worry about her. Spend that energy coming up with a good punishment." He half-rose and hugged me, whispering in my ear, "Even if I know you'll worry anyway."

I hugged him back and got to my feet. "I should take off."

"I'll bring out my truck," Reese said. "Just wait in the drive."

I paused, momentarily confused before remembering that he was coming with me. I hesitated, ready to tell him no, I'd go alone, which meant no one could see how fast I drove, but I squelched the urge. It was really better if I didn't get behind the wheel of a motor vehicle right now.

"Hold up, and I'll grab my bag," Nick said.

I turned to him and it felt like moving through molasses, every word someone spoke taking ten seconds to penetrate and another ten to process.

"No need for that, Nicky," Antonio said. "Katie's just wandered off. Clay will find her before Elena gets there."

Nick opened his mouth.

"No need," Antonio said, his tone firmer. He glanced at me and nodded. "Unless the Alpha wants you there."

A reminder, maybe unintentional, but I felt the kick in the ass and appreciated it. *Take control here.*

I straightened. "No, there's no need for anyone else to come. If Clay doesn't find her, Reese and I will join the search. That's enough."

A subtle throat clearing and I looked to see Morgan hovering in the doorway, keeping himself a little apart as usual.

"If you did want one more nose," he said. "Mine's not as good as yours but…"

Morgan had spent a year living primarily in wolf form in the Alaskan wilderness. His nose wasn't spectacular but his wilderness tracking was.

"Any weekend plans?" I asked.

"Doesn't matter. This is more important. At the very least, I can keep Reese company on the drive back and switch off if he gets tired."

"All right then. Grab your stuff."

Five

CLAY DIDN'T CALL, which meant he hadn't found her. If he called just to check in, I'd have thought he had news, and then I'd be in worse shape when I found out otherwise. When we got within a half hour of the cabin, I texted, letting him know I was almost there and that Reese and Morgan were with me. Ten minutes later, he replied with, "OK." That was it. OK.

We were on the last road when a figure stepped from the woods, far ahead. Blue jeans, T-shirt, blond hair. I knew it was Clay even before a smaller blond figure joined him.

Logan raised a hand in greeting. Clay just stood by the side of the road, hands stuffed in his pockets, face turned away, as if watching for someone coming from the other direction. When the truck drew close, he stepped back into the tree shadows. Logan darted forward and Clay lunged, grabbing him by the shoulder, as if he'd been about to run in front of us. Even when Logan had been young enough to make that mistake, he'd never truly been young enough to make it. But now Clay grabbed him.

Clay let Logan go as Reese pulled over. Logan was there before I got out of the car, his arms going around me in a tight hug, as he said, "I'm glad you're here, Momma," and it took me a moment to hug him back, because all I could think was, "This is Kate's job." Kate was the one who'd race out to greet us after a trip. Who'd throw herself into our arms, often literally. Logan would follow but stand back and wait for his greeting hug. Now, as I embraced him, he melted into my arms in a way he hadn't since he was little, collapsing there with his face against me. That hug told me more than anything that he was as lost as his sister right now. Lost without her.

"She's out there," he said when he finally pulled back. "She's okay. I'd know if she wasn't."

It was true. They shared a bond, enough to sense when the other was hurt. A rarely-tested bond, because it was rare for them to be far enough apart not to *witness* the other get hurt.

"Go see Dad," Logan whispered. "He's not doing so well."

I nodded and turned to Reese. "Could you—?"

Reese was already leaning over the passenger seat. "Hey, bud. Bet you haven't had lunch."

Logan climbed into the truck without a word.

Once the truck drove away, I crossed the road. Clay stayed where he was, hidden in the shadows, but I could see enough to know that Logan was right. He wasn't doing well. I hadn't expected him to be. I'd had nightmares of this myself for years now, of taking the kids someplace innocent, like the park or the mall. Taking two children. Coming home with one. In those nightmares, I stood outside Stonehaven, and I couldn't go in. Couldn't face Clay. Couldn't tell him what happened. What I'd done, because even if I wasn't to blame, I'd still taken our two children out and returned with one, and that would forever be my fault.

They say the loss of a child can break the strongest marriage. Clay and I have overcome more than any normal couple. We've endured more, and we came out stronger, more tightly bonded than ever. Yet if there was one thing that I considered a truly possible threat to that bond, it was this. Having to walk up to him and say, "I lost one of our children."

When Clay turned, I saw that in his face. A look that said he had no idea how to deal with this, to comprehend the possibility of it. When I saw that, I knew I was wrong. Whatever happened, if "it" ever happened, I wouldn't lose him over it. I would never let that happen.

I walked to him, and I put my arms around his neck, and he hugged me so tight my ribs crackled.

"I'm sor—" he began.

"No," I said, and cut him off with a kiss, long and deep, and when I pulled back and he tried again to apologize, I said, "No," harsher now, kissing him harder.

"The only person to blame here is Kate," I said. "And when we find her, I'm going to blame her so hard she won't ever forget it."

"I didn't know she'd left until—"

"You're her father, not her jailer." I looked him in the eye. "We always said we wouldn't overdo it, but when Logan called me earlier, I knew we had. They understand how scared we are of something happening to them. We have pounded that into their heads since they were old enough to listen. There is no way in hell that Kate can say she didn't know how worried we'd be. She's punishing us, and when I find her..." I sucked in breath. "I don't even know what I'll do, but she will understand that this is not the way to punish us. Not ever."

Clay's gaze swung back to the forest. "She's out there. No one's taken her. Logan's right about that." A wan quirk of his lips that couldn't quite be called a smile. "And we really shouldn't have to rely on our eight-year-old son to be the voice of reason."

"Which is where I think we've overdone it. I'm all for honesty. I'm all for protecting our children. I'm definitely all for making sure they never doubt how important they are to

us. But kids shouldn't know their parents are that *scared* of anything."

He pulled me into a hug again, sharp and fierce, his voice more his own as he said, "I'm not going to apologize, darling. I know you don't want to hear that. But I'm sorry you had to get that call. I'd have done anything to avoid that."

"I know." I squeezed him back. "But she's good at running and hiding, apparently. Takes after her mom."

"Not so much running and hiding as getting pissed off and storming out. Which *does* seem familiar."

"Thanks."

The briefest smile. "Hey, I never said you didn't have good reason. That's where this is different. She's angry because you were delayed for one day on legitimate Pack business, and because her brother gave her hell for getting pissy with me. Neither justifies taking off."

"It does when you're a teenager."

"She's eight."

"I know. That's what scares me." I took his hand as we walked into the forest. "Bring me up to speed."

Logan had been the one who discovered Kate was missing. He'd known Clay would be planning to get them up early and off to meet me at the airport. Not realizing my flight had been delayed, Logan had set his alarm to wake up at five and surprise Clay with breakfast. He'd gone into Kate's room to see if she wanted to help—his apology for giving her shit plus a chance for her to apologize for doing the same to her dad.

Kate hadn't been in her room. Logan had searched the cabin. Then he'd alerted Clay.

Clay and Logan had both figured Kate had stepped out for a dawn walk, hoping to incite a mild panic attack and repay her father for imagined slights. Clay had Changed and followed her trail from her bedroom into the forest.

"She went straight for the stream," he said.

"So you couldn't track her."

He nodded. "That's when I started to worry. Also when I started getting pissed off. Going for a walk to spook me is bad enough. Intentionally hiding her trail to *panic* me?" He shook his head. "I keep thinking how childish that is. And then I think, 'Yeah, because she's a *child*.'"

"Easy to forget that sometimes."

"True. This is beyond childish. It feels…"

"Vindictive?"

He made a face and rolled his shoulders. That wasn't a word he wanted to use for his little girl, but it fit under the circumstances, as hard as it was for either of us to admit it.

After a moment, he said, "I keep thinking maybe there's more to it, maybe someone's…" Another roll of his shoulders. "But there's no sign of that. I can't even blame sleepwalking, because taking off her shoes and tramping through the stream is a conscious act. No one lured her out. She just left."

"Which means she's out there, and we'll get her back."

He nodded and continued his story, telling me that he'd gone all the way to where the stream emptied into a lake, and there'd been no exit trail on either bank. That didn't mean she'd swam into the lake. Not fully dressed. She must have left the stream at some point, and her diluted scent wasn't strong enough for him to pick up. That was where I'd come in. My nose, at least.

Six

CLAY STAYED IN the woods to keep searching. I'd head back to the cabin to give the others my game plan. Yes, I could just phone Reese, but I wanted Logan to hear it too, reassuring him his parents had this under control, as they should.

My phone rang as I was jogging back. I checked it. Jeremy. Shit.

We hadn't told him about Kate—we didn't want to alarm him. But if I spoke to him, no matter how hard I played "situation normal," he'd know something was wrong.

I should just let him leave a message and pretend we were busy and...

I stared at his name on my screen, and I felt my thumb move to the Answer button. It wasn't an impulse to obey my former Alpha. In the past, I obeyed Jeremy because I trusted and respected him. But now, as I hit that button, an entirely different impulse drove me. The one where I was scared shitless and desperately wanted to speak to the one person who might be able to calm me down, the person who'd been there when Clay bit me, who'd been there for me ever since.

I answered with a casual, "Hey," telling myself I wouldn't alarm him unnecessarily. I'd take whatever comfort I could get from simply speaking to him.

"Good, you're there."

"What's up?"

"Nothing. I just wanted to touch base, see if you'd gotten to the cabin all right."

"Sorry. You're wondering what happened in London, right? I should have called. I've just been—"

"I wouldn't check up on you, Elena. You're on vacation, and if you needed my help with the British situation, you would have called. This really is simply a check-in."

He was lying. It's taken years for me to learn how to tell. Jeremy lies better than anyone I know. More smoothly, anyway. It's a survival skill, necessary for growing up with a bastard like Malcolm for a father. In person, Jeremy gives no cues. But when I can't see him, I can hear the faint signs in his voice, a slightly too casual air. Not unlike Logan. There might be no blood bond there, but Jeremy was as much a force in the twins' lives as their parents, and Logan in particular has "inherited" a few of his mannerisms.

"So everything's okay?" I said.

"Of course. And there? How are the kids?"

I hesitated.

"Elena?"

"Logan's at the house with Reese, who drove me up. Kate, Clay and I are out for a walk." All technically true.

"Is Kate with you right now then?"

"Not this second. I'm by myself."

"She's with Clay then?"

Had Antonio called Jeremy and told him? After all, they'd been best friends since Jeremy was old enough to sit up in his crib. But notifying Jeremy would undercut my authority with the Pack, and if Antonio had disagreed with me about not informing Jeremy, he'd have let me know.

"What's wrong?" I asked carefully.

"Does something have to be wrong for me to call? I'm guessing that your meeting with Parker did not go well, and you've had a long flight and drive—"

"Yes, I'm in a shitty mood. But if you're suggesting I'm being testy and paranoid, and then I find out later you *weren't* just calling to check in…"

He sighed. "I think I preferred the old days. You never talked to me that way when I was Alpha."

"Sure I did. And you appreciated it just as much then as you do now, because other than Tonio I'm the only one who'll call you on your bullshit. What's up?"

"I would just like to know if Kate's all right."

"Did someone suggest otherwise?"

A pause.

"Jeremy?" I said. "If one of the guys went behind my back and contacted you, I need to know that."

"And I would tell you because I would agree. I have not had any communication with anyone since Clayton called last night to say you were going to miss your connecting flight. I'm asking about Kate because..." He cleared his throat. "I saw something."

I stopped short. "A vision? About Kate?"

"I...don't know. I was reading, and I drifted off, and...I'm presuming it was a dream. All I want is to confirm that she's there."

Visions were part of the bonus pack Jeremy gets from having kitsune blood. He sees his Pack in danger or, if we're missing, visions that could help him find us. Which should seem he'd be the first person Clay would call when Kate disappeared. Except his powers didn't work with the twins. Maybe they were too young. Or maybe it meant that, despite the fact they'd shown secondary characteristics, they didn't have enough supernatural blood.

Whatever the reason, it bothered Jeremy. To him, his inability to see them felt like a failure of will. His power worked with his longtime girlfriend, a necromancer. Obviously the emotional bond was there with the twins, so why not the psychic link? That was why we hadn't notified him. He would try to make that connection and feel guilty when he couldn't.

"Elena?" His voice crackled down the line. "Where's Kate?"

I told him. When I finished, I said, "I know no one's taken her. There's absolutely no sign of that. She just left. But..." I inhaled. "It's been at least six hours, Jer. Six hours in the forest. If she could come back, she..." I couldn't finish.

"I'm on my way."

I listened to the jangle of keys and thump of shoes pulled on as he left the house without so much as a pause for breath. I said nothing to slow him down. Nor did he hang up, instead holding me on the line until the car engine roared to life, and I asked, "What did you see?"

A pause so long I thought he'd left the phone on only by accident.

"Jer?"

"I don't know," he said finally. "It wasn't anything useful."

"Can you tell me anyway? Please?"

"I saw Kate. That's it. There wasn't a setting. It was just her, sitting somewhere. She was..."

I waited almost a whole minute for him to finish. Then, "Jeremy, please. What was she—?"

"She was crying." He hurried on. "But she didn't sound hurt. Just confused and scared. Not frightened. Not like there was anyone else there. Just..."

"Lost?"

He exhaled. "Yes, exactly. She seemed lost. She looked fine. Dirty, but fine. She's lost in the woods, and if it was another child, that would be cause for panic, but she's your daughter and Clay's. That means she's smart and she's resourceful. More than that, it means she has an entire Pack of werewolves who can scour those woods looking for her. She's not lost in the Alaskan wilderness. It's a limited area. It's summer, there's fresh water and no predators. We'll find her before she's in any physical danger."

✶

YES, I'D RATHER Jeremy had said he'd seen Kate asleep in her bed, having snuck back while everyone was out searching. Or seen her at a picnic table, conveniently located beside a sign with the park's name. Hell, I'd have settled for, "She's skipping stones in the water, but I can't tell exactly where." Some proof that she was fine and just being a brat.

But Jeremy was right. While lost and scared would be a traumatic experience, this was a problem we could solve. No one had taken her. Jeremy was phoning Antonio and telling him to bring Nick and Noah up. Karl lived in Philly, putting him an extra three hours south, but I called him as soon as I got off the phone with Jeremy. Hope was coming too, after they dropped Nita off at her grandmother's. As a chaos half-demon, Hope might not have a nose for scents, but she had one for trouble, which meant she might be able to find a lost and frightened little girl.

So we had a plan. Kate was out there, and we would find her. It was just a matter of doing the work.

I sent Morgan to search the far side of the stream. Reese and Logan would stick together close to the cabin, in case she came back. Once I'd given them their orders, I went back to Clay, Changed into a wolf and began scouring the banks of the stream.

Two hours later, I figured out why I couldn't find an exit trail for Kate. Unfortunately, I couldn't explain it to Clay while I was in wolf form.

Twenty years of Changing forms at least once a week has increased my pain threshold. It's not ever going to get easier, but it's no longer an ordeal and I usually bounce back fast. That day, though, I lay in the clearing, curled in a ball, shivering despite the hot August day.

"Elena?" Clay poked his head into the clearing. "Shit!"

He pushed his way past the brambles as I forced myself to sit up.

"I'm fine," I said. "Just need a little extra recuperation time. Not enough sleep."

"Or food, I bet. When's the last time you ate?"

"I will." I started to press to my feet, but a wave of exhaustion stopped me and I settled onto the ground, as if that had been my plan all along. "I know why we can't find the trail."

"Okay, but when did you eat?"

"Stop that," I snapped. "This is important."

"No shit. So is the fact that you're ready to pass out—"

"I'm fine. Kate climbed a tree. There are plenty overhanging the stream. The forest is dense enough that she..." I blinked, and it was as if someone had yanked the thought from my head. "She..."

"She moved through the trees," Clay said. "Far enough that we wouldn't pick up her trail near the stream. Got that. We'll widen the search grid. After you eat."

"I'm not—"

"You haven't eaten since Logan called you nearly seven hours ago. I doubt you did more than grab a bagel in the airport when you landed. Meaning you—"

"I'm fine."

"—meaning you have Changed twice in an hour, with a blood sugar level probably near zero. You're going to sit there while I go grab food, and you're not leaving this clearing until I come back."

I glowered up at him. "I'm not a child."

His cheek ticked, temper rising. "I—"

"And don't say I'm acting like one either."

"No." The word came slowly, with forced calm. "You aren't acting like a child. You're acting like a mother whose child is missing, and who doesn't want to waste time on something as inconsequential as eating. And I'm the guy telling you it won't be inconsequential if you pass out, and we won't find her any faster if you're unconscious."

I pressed my palms against my eyes. "You're right. I'm sorry. I just—"

"I know." He crouched and embraced me. "But I need to get you food, and if you go looking for Kate while I'm gone…"

"I'll pass out in the forest, and you'll have to search for both of us. You're right. Go. Just…"

"I'll run."

"Sorry, I don't mean—"

"I'll run. Give me ten minutes, fifteen tops. If you can grab a few minutes' shut-eye, it'll help, but I won't expect it."

He took off at a lope. Once he was gone, I did lie down. I had to, before I fell over. But as woozy as I felt, I couldn't keep my eyes shut long enough to drift off.

I was lying there when my phone rang. I reached over and tugged it out of my jeans. I checked the screen. Private Caller. Then the time.

"Goddamn it," I muttered. "Not this—"

I stopped. It was six *local* time. *Eastern* time. The other calls had been six Greenwich Mean time. I remembered the caller's words and my gut went cold.

"No," I whispered.

I scrambled to hit Answer.

"Who—?" I began, more squeak than word.

"It's six o'clock. Do you know where your puppy is?"

"Wait!" I said. The line disconnected. I hit Call Back. Of course it didn't go through.

I staggered to my feet and shot from the clearing. ⌒

Seven

I RAN THROUGH THE woods. Naked. I just ran, vines grabbing my feet, branches lashing my face, no more thinking of finding a path than of taking my clothes. The world dipped and shimmered, and I heard Clay's voice, warning about my blood sugar. Yet I kept going, a stumbling, staggering run, telling myself I could do it, the cabin wasn't far, just keep going, tell Clay, warn Clay, I could pass out once he knew.

Kate.

Oh God, Kate.

Do you know where your puppy is?

Leaves crackled under my feet. I slipped, but righted myself fast. A distant shout penetrated the throbbing in my head, and I slowed for a single step before realizing it was Reese, calling for Kate, and I pitched forward again and—

And black.

✒

GET UP. COME on, *damn you. Get up!*

The words whispered past in my own voice. I struggled to rise to them, only to be pulled back under.

Darkness. Crawling through darkness.

Then a scent.

I know that scent.

I jolted upright. I was sitting on the forest floor, naked, and it took several seconds before I remembered why. I reached out to push up. My hand touched down on something hard yet yielding. I turned to see my hand resting on a plain white running shoe.

I struggled to focus on that shoe, but the world threatened to short out again, darkness rising. A voice sounded behind me. My own voice.

"*Let's get you better shoes than that.*"

"*I like these.*"

"*And while I appreciate the frugality, Kate, they won't last as long as a decent pair. There's a sports store in the mall. We'll get you—*"

"*I want these.*"

"*Why?*"

Logan's voice, exasperated. "Because the other girls make fun of her for them. They call her a scholarship kid because she doesn't wear name brands. She's being contrary."

"*Maybe I like being called a scholarship kid.*"

"*But you aren't," I said.*

"*They don't need to know that. And I could be. I'm not as smart as Logan, but my grades are good enough that I could be a scholarship kid. They couldn't. I want these shoes.*"

The memory faded and my fingers wrapped around the shoe. So I'd passed out exactly where Kate had dropped a shoe?

No, that wasn't possible. Someone left this beside me.

A smell drifted past. The smell of a scent blocker. I pushed up then, still clutching Kate's shoe as I looked around and inhaled deeply.

He's here.

I blinked hard, pushing past the sensation that I was going to dead-drop to the ground again. I could feel the aches and bruises from my last fall, but I paid them no mind, focused instead on that scent.

I crouched. When I lowered my head to sniff the ground, the world dipped into black, but only for a moment. I found the scent blocker. That was all, though. I inhaled as deeply as I could. Those sprays and washes weren't perfect. I should be able to—

There. I found it. But faint. So incredibly faint that all I could detect was human scent.

No, there was more. The barest touch of musk. Of werewolf. I growled under my breath. *Tell me something I don't know. Give me more, damn it.*

The crackle of undergrowth. I shot up so fast I staggered sideways and grabbed a sapling before I fell.

"Reese? Morgan?"

Silence answered. Then the crack of a twig. Deliberate. Drawing me out. I stepped around a tree and peered into the forest. It was still early evening, and our day vision is no better than a human's. I relied on my nose and ears, straining for—

A crinkle of dried leaf. More whisper than crackle. As if someone picked it up and intentionally crumpled it. My hands clenched at my sides.

I wasn't in any shape for this. I could barely walk, let alone fight. Why the hell hadn't I grabbed food from the cabin?

Because all I could think about was Kate. Nothing else mattered.

I'd spent my adulthood winnowing out weakness. Examining my life for every chink that a mutt could use to get at me. But there are some weaknesses you can't fix. Not without cutting out your heart. Not without consigning yourself to a life that isn't worth living.

Another broken twig.

Come and get me.

I turned away from the sound, the movement physically painful, as if I was turning my back on Kate herself.

He has her. You need to go to him, save her.

I can't. Not like this. I just can't.

I'd heard Reese. Which direction...? Yes, there. His scent on the breeze, Logan's mingling with it.

If I took off, I could lose my pursuer. Or, worse, I could lure him to my son when I was in no condition to fight.

Reese could fight.

But well enough to bet my child's life on?

I reached for my phone to text Reese. That is a testament to exactly how exhausted I was. Given that I was naked, I certainly didn't have my phone. Which meant I couldn't warn Reese to send Logan to the house. Couldn't help Kate unless I led her captor to her brother.

Kate was missing. In danger. Logan was safe. With Reese. To save her, I could justify the risk of leading her captor to him, because Reese was there, and I was there, and Logan himself was there, and as much as I wanted to think of him as my baby, my innocent and defenseless child, he hadn't been either for a very long time. That was a life for human children. Not mine.

I started in the direction I'd heard Reese. I moved slowly, looking about as if discombobulated. It wasn't entirely an act.

Walking felt like swimming through cotton. Focusing on my task took effort. Hell, putting one foot in front of the other took effort. Too much stress. Too little sleep. Too little food. Damn it, I had to be more careful. I really, really had—

The forest had gone quiet behind me. I slowed and strained to listen.

Dead leaves crunched underfoot. I pretended to scan the forest. I knew what direction the sound came from, but if my pursuer figured that out, he'd know I was leading him somewhere. So I peered about, blinking and staggering— and trying not to actually fall over. Then I feigned catching another noise, in the direction I wanted to lead him.

I took two steps and my phone rang. My distant, abandoned phone. It was my "general" ringtone, meaning it could be the guy pursuing me.

I turned around. I moved too fast and stumbled. The world constricted, like a peephole closing, and I fell to one knee. I pushed up, again moving too fast, pitching forward now.

Someone laughed.

I twisted to look back and saw a figure hidden in the shadow of a tree. He turned and started to walk away.

"No!" I shouted, before I could stop myself.

The man broke into a slow jog. I ran for him. I stumbled twice, then dropped to one knee again, pitching forward, hands hitting the ground and breaking my fall.

He turned. From this distance, all I could make out was a figure dressed in some sort of jumpsuit, with the hood pulled up and dark shades over his eyes. He watched me, crouched there, breathing hard, struggling to stay conscious.

I needed to go after him. He had Kate. He'd taken her and—

That's not what Jeremy saw.

Then he saw wrong. He misinterpreted.

Jeremy? No.

When he'd seen Kate, she was alone and scared and lost. Not captured. That would have shown on her face, rage mingled with fear.

But that was hours ago. Anything could have happened since then.

The man took a step toward me. Then another. I tensed, muscles bunching, but even as my body prepared for attack, it screamed in protest. I didn't have the energy. I absolutely did not.

So I'd run? Leave him with Kate, if he had her? Bring help and hope we picked up his trail when even now, downwind, I smelled nothing?

There was a third alternative. It just took my exhausted brain a moment to find it. When I did, I turned and started loping in the other direction, as fast as I could safely manage. I glanced back to see him hesitating.

Good. Reconsider, then go back to Kate before I bring help. And as soon as you turn around, I'm coming after you...at my own pace. I'll see where you go, and then I'll get help.

I continued on. When I looked again, he'd resumed following me.

Damn it!

Even the force of the mental curse, resounding in my skull, was enough to make the world tilt. I squeezed my eyes shut.

Back to plan one. Lead him to Reese.

"Hey!" Reese's voice echoed through the woods so suddenly that I thought I'd imagined it.

"Logan?" he called. "Where are you?"

No. No, no, no.

I glanced over my shoulder. The man was coming faster now, his gaze turned in the direction of that voice. I started to run. I didn't think. I broke into a full-out run toward Reese, every bit of energy I had left pouring into it. Just run, just get to—

Everything went dark. ⁀

Eight

SOMEONE WAS THERE. Above me. I struggled toward consciousness, but I couldn't find it. I lay there, too weak to open my eyes, too weak to sustain thought, forgetting why I'd woken, then catching that vague sense of a presence.

Bare fingers touched my arm.

Got to get up. *Got to get up.*

A scent wafted past and my whole body convulsed with recognition. I tried to leap up and felt the abyss threaten.

No, please no. I need to—

The abyss of unconsciousness opened again and I tumbled in, one last thought before I lost consciousness, my brain snagging on the name, holding it until the last possible moment.

Malcolm.

*

I WOKE TO a figure looming over me, fingers on my arm. I shot up, knocking the hand back, snarling as my nostrils filled with that scent and—

"Shhh," a voice whispered. "You're all right, Elena. It's just me."

Just me.

No, I smelled...

I couldn't remember. There'd been something... Someone... But now all I smelled was a familiar and welcome scent.

I opened my eyes to see Jeremy crouched beside me, his fingers still on my arm, squeezing now. He pushed something bright and colorful at me.

"Drink this."

A juice box. When I saw it, my brain tumbled backward, to the grocery store, shopping for our trip.

"That's the wrong kind," Logan said. *"It's not real juice."*

"I don't want real juice," Kate replied.

"Why not? It tastes better, and it's better for you."

Kate, rolling her eyes. "You're such an old man. You should try being a kid, Lo. This might help." She threw the fruit punch into the cart, sighing as Logan added a pure juice blend.

I scrambled up. "Logan!"

Jeremy's hand tightened on my arm. "He's fine."

"No, Reese was looking for him. I heard—"

"If he was, then I'm sure it lasted about three seconds. Logan doesn't wander off. You know that."

You're such an old man. You should try being a kid.

There were times I worried that Kate was right, that my son was too old for his age, too mature. And there were times, like this, when I was so very glad of it.

"Drink."

I drained the box and felt the sugar spread, my mind focusing.

"Kate," I said. "She—"

"Everyone's looking for her."

Jeremy pushed another box at me, straw punched through.

"There's something else…" *What had I been thinking about when I woke up? A person, wasn't it?* "It's important."

"Drink."

I did. More syrupy-sweet fruit punch. The crackle of undergrowth, as loud as a gunshot, and I didn't need to look up to know who it was. I managed a smile as Clay barreled through, my clothing bunched in his arms.

"Thought I heard your voice," he said.

I nodded. "I'm sorry. I…"

My brain started gaining traction, remembering why I'd left the clearing, but it couldn't quite grab hold of the memory.

I'd been in the clearing. Then I'd heard Reese, and I'd been worried about Logan and...

No, there was more to it. In the middle. And afterward. What had it been? A person...

I took the third proffered drink box and worked on it, slower now.

"I passed out," I said. "Fainted."

"Low blood sugar and possibly dehydration," Jeremy said. "Add stress and exhaustion..."

"I know," I said. "I was careless. And stupid."

"No, just worried."

Clay crouched beside me and held out my clothing. I pulled on my shirt. As I did, I could feel the sugar inching through my veins, fuel slowly working down the lines toward the engine.

"There was someone out here," I said. "I was following... No, he was following— Shit." I pressed my hands against my face. "That was really, really stupid. I passed out with someone right there. I could have—"

I caught a glimpse of Clay's expression and stopped. No need to put that possibility into words. I could have been killed. Easily. All because I hadn't gotten enough to eat. Beyond stupid.

"Someone was out here?" Clay said. "With you? I didn't catch a scent."

74

I had.

Whose scent?

I couldn't remember.

"Elena?" Clay's hands on my knees as I sat up. "Is someone here?"

"I only saw a figure. He was wearing a jumpsuit and hood. The jumpsuit... Shit!" I squeezed my eyes shut and shook my head. "His scent. A carbon-lined jumpsuit to cover his scent."

Clay rose. "I'm going to scout. See if I can pick up tracks. I won't go far." He bent again, in front of me. "You're okay?"

I nodded. "Go scout. Please." A few gears on my brain started turning. I looked at Jeremy. "Can you text the others? Warn them? Tell Reese to get Logan back inside the cabin. I'd help, but my phone..."

Something about my phone... Can't remember.

"My phone's back in the clearing."

"Nope," Clay said. "Right there." He pointed at the clothing pile and managed a tired smile. "But feel free to get Jer to play messenger. Payback for all the times you had to do it."

Clay left. I pulled my phone from the pile as Jeremy started texting on his. I knew he'd contact Reese first, so I said, "I'll get Morgan. Is Nick in yet or—"

I stopped as I turned on my phone and saw the missed call. Private Caller. The reason I'd fled the clearing slammed back.

"The call," I said.

Jeremy looked up from his phone. I was yanking at my jeans, fumbling to pull them on. He put his hand out.

"Slow down, Elena. What call?"

I kept dressing. "When I was in England, I got two calls at six o'clock their time. Pranks, it seemed. Asking if I knew where my puppy was."

"Puppy?" His eyes widened. Jeremy checked his watch. "He called again? Today at six?"

I nodded as I snapped a band around my ponytail. "Six *our* time. It was a child's voice. A boy's. A singsong, so I don't know if there was an accent, but the voice was the same every time, which means I think it was a recording. He called again while I was running back to the cabin. There's no message though."

"Text? E-mail?"

"No, nothing. Can you call Morgan and Antonio?" I started to leap up. "Karl, too. I need—"

Jeremy grabbed my wrist. "You need to slow down."

I tried to shake him off, but he held tight and handed me another juice box. "Slow down and think, Elena. For Kate's sake, you need to focus."

"I am focused. She's out there—"

"Captured? I didn't see that. Yes, I could be wrong, but think of it this way: all he's done is phone you with a recording. If he had her, wouldn't he send a photo? Text a message? Have her talk to you?"

"Maybe that's what he was trying to do the last time. Have her speak to me."

"But you had him in your sights."

"Then there are two of them," I snapped.

"True, that doesn't mean she *isn't* captured, but we have no proof she is, and even if she was, racing into that forest won't help. You've been doing that for hours. You, Clay, Morgan..."

I rubbed my face and concentrated on his words. "Right. We need a plan. There's no reason to panic..."

Yes, there is. There's more. Something you're forgetting.

"Elena?"

I drained the juice box and closed my eyes, struggling to capture a memory determined to elude me.

A smell...

I'd woken to a smell.

No, that was Jeremy.

But I'd thought it wasn't. Who did I think it had been? Why couldn't I remember?

I couldn't. I just couldn't. And every moment I spent chasing that memory was another moment I wasn't chasing Kate.

I texted Morgan and called a group meeting at the cabin. ⌒

Nine

BY THE TIME I dressed and returned to the cabin, everyone was there except Karl and Hope. I pulled up an area map on my laptop. The forest was about five square miles. That doesn't sound big, but when you're trying to find one little girl, it's huge. I divvied it up into linear strips. Then I split the group.

Reese would stay at the cabin with Logan in case Kate came back. They'd also cook dinner, for anyone who got hungry and needed a break.

Morgan would be on his own. That was his preference, and I knew better than to fight it. Nick with Noah, Antonio and Clay on their own, and me with Jeremy. I could see that Jeremy thought I'd made a mistake there. He should track on his own and put Clay with me. But my gut said Jeremy shouldn't be by himself. Clay and I would travel parallel, though, close enough to shout to each other. Jeremy seemed satisfied with that. I may have been Alpha for three years now, but the training wheels were still on, and I felt better when he approved a plan.

It was getting dark by the time we set out again. For those in pairs, one person would stay in human form, with a flashlight, while the other Changed. I'd had two more juice boxes on the way back to the cabin, eaten half a loaf of bread with half a pound of cold cuts while I'd talked to the others, and then ate three granola bars on the way to our search strip. So lack of energy for Changing wasn't a problem.

Jeremy and I had gone along our strip and back once, and we were halfway down the next section when we reached a cabin. It was the first we'd spotted. There was an abundance of better cottage land in Vermont, on the mountains and along the lakes. This patch of forest was all rocky foothills with little to recommend it except privacy, which made it exactly what we'd wanted for our family vacation.

Jeremy and I were in one of the least populated sections, the ground too uneven, the main road too far. But there was this one cottage, which wouldn't even meet the standards of our rental website. From a distance, I'd thought it was abandoned. As I drew close, I could see signs of seasonal habitation. Hunting season, I'd guess, given the primitive-ness of it.

I told Jeremy I was going to check out the cabin. I didn't actually *say* that. If there's a wolf language, werewolves have never mastered it. What we have—and what I suspect real wolves have—is a communication system based on a combination of sound and body language. A bark means pay attention. A howl means, "I'm here." A growl means, "Go away." Any longtime dog owner is probably as adept at deciphering the language as we are. My yips to Jeremy meant something like, "Don't worry, I'm not in trouble and I don't need you to come here—I'm just getting your attention so you see what I'm up to, which in this case is checking out this cabin." He waved the flashlight, telling me he got it and wouldn't stray too far.

The cottage was one-and-a-half stories with a loft. It was big, maybe a couple of thousand feet. The wood had turned a grayish color under a patina of moss. There was no yard. No gardens or any landscaping at all. Just a rutted dirt drive leading from a road too distant for me to see. There was a welcome sign on the porch, though, along with a couple of Adirondack chairs. Signs of occupancy. Hopefully not cur-rent occupancy.

I snuffled along the drive. I could pick up the stink of anti-freeze and motor oil, but it was old, soaked into the dirt.

I continued up what passed for a front walk—a path through the undergrowth. There were human scents here, but again, old. I hopped onto the porch and stopped at the front door. More snuffling. No recent human scents.

I hopped down and rounded the cabin. No sign of a side door. I put my nose down and continued along the wall. Around the back and—

A breeze-swept scent crept along the ground.

I lurched forward, as if I was back in the forest with my blood sugar nearly nil. One leg buckled as I staggered toward the door. I growled and righted myself and continued forward and…

The scent wafted up from the earth and my head shot down, nose to the ground, dry dirt filling my nostrils as I inhaled so hard I started wheezing. But the smell was still there, threaded through the dirt. I dropped to my belly, muzzle on the ground, eyes squeezed shut as I inhaled it.

Kate.

I lay there for a moment, breathing in her scent, my head filled with nothing else. Then I opened my eyes and blinked hard. Another moment to orient myself and I rose, snorting and huffing, clearing my nose. I lowered it as I snuffled around the rear door.

Kate's scent. No one else's. Just my daughter. Which meant—

Which meant nothing when I already knew her pursuer was taking steps to cover his smell. He could be inside with her.

My hackles rose, a growl reverberating through me before I swallowed it back.

I looked up at the closed door. Without fingers, I wasn't getting it open myself. I needed to—

Clay.

I needed to get Clay. Not to solve this problem, but because I'd smelled our daughter and I had to tell him right away. I turned and ran into the forest. Then I stopped. If I went to him, I could tell him quietly, without alerting anyone. But I'd also be out of sight of the cabin.

"Elena!" It was Jeremy, far enough off that I couldn't see him. "Elena!"

Well, that eliminated the stealth option. I threw back my head and howled for Clay.

When I heard crashing through the forest, I thought, "That was fast." But it was the wrong sort of crashing—the kind that came from someone on two legs. I caught the scent and snorted, certain I was mistaken.

Jeremy? He never made that much noise.

I saw his figure coming through the trees as Clay's answering howl reached me. I replied, which meant, "Yes, I mean you. Come here."

"Elena, no!" Jeremy shot through into the clearing. He ran to me, hands out. "Stop!"

I did, but it was too late. Clay had given a half-howl, half-yip back, saying he was on his way. I looked up at Jeremy, poised there, catching his breath.

"I smelled—"

I cut him off with a grunt—"I know"—and walked to the back door, making a show of sniffing there. When he caught the scent, his eyes widened.

"Kate? No, that's not who I—" Jeremy's eyes narrowed as he scanned the forest. "Do you smell anyone else?"

I sniffed the ground and shook my head. Then I lifted my muzzle, inhaled and shook my head again. I wanted to add that I didn't expect to smell anyone, given the jumpsuit, but there was no way of communicating that.

"Did Kate go in the house?"

I arched my brows as best I could manage in wolf form. Jeremy wasn't given to stupid questions, and as soon as I answered, I got a better look at his expression. His slightly widened eyes held a touch of panic, and the fur on my back rose as a growl vibrated through me.

Distant paws pounded the earth, the rhythmic sound I knew well. When Jeremy looked up, though, he tensed. I started to run toward Clay.

"Elena! No!"

I reached the forest's edge before skidding to a stop. That's when the breeze slid past, with a scent so faint that for a moment, I thought I was smelling Jeremy. And as soon as I thought that, my brain tumbled back to waking in the clearing, thinking I detected a scent that bore notes in common with Jeremy's—the smell of a familial bond.

Malcolm.

Ten

ARLIER, LYING IN that clearing when I'd passed out, someone had come and bent beside me and I'd smelled Malcolm and when I woke, I'd forgotten.

I turned on Jeremy, snarling, every hair on my body raised.

"You smell Malcolm," Jeremy said. "I know."

I snarled again, snapping now.

"And I should have mentioned that quicker. I'm sorry." Jeremy brushed his hair from his face.

If Kate's disappearance could short out my mental facilities, Malcolm's reappearance could do the same to his son. Clay might joke about being psychotic; Malcolm was. He'd made Jeremy's life hell, largely because Jeremy wasn't what Malcolm would consider a proper werewolf. In short, Jeremy wasn't Clay. When Clay came along, that had only complicated matters, because Clay had made it clear, from the time he was a child, that Jeremy was *his* Alpha in every way. Malcolm might aspire to be Alpha, but to Clay, he'd never be more than the son of a bitch they were stuck with until Clay was old enough to kill him without Jeremy knowing.

That had never happened. Clay had grown, and Jeremy had beat Malcolm for Alphahood, and then Malcolm had exiled himself from Pack life. By the time Clay would have been ready to take on a wolf of Malcolm's stature, the bastard was dead. Or so it had seemed for nearly thirty years, until he'd turned up in Nast Cabal custody. Clay had then reverted to plan A, with my full endorsement. Kill Malcolm before Jeremy found out he was alive.

That hadn't worked so well, as Hollis Parker had pointed out. Malcolm had eluded us until Nick took him down and Vanessa planted the tracking device, which made him easy to find but no easier to kill. So we'd had to tell Jeremy. No way in hell were we taking the chance that Malcolm would come after him.

Holding off even that long had been tough on both Clay and me, and we still questioned whether we'd made the right choice. Jeremy certainly didn't think so. He hadn't gotten angry. Jeremy didn't get angry. He'd shut us out—just closed down and taken a two-week trip with Jaime.

Clay and I can handle anger. That's a language we speak fluently. Silence, though? Even the memory sent a chill through me. Yet as I watched Jeremy's face, his expression shell-shocked, I did not think we made the wrong choice. We'd owed it to him to try and keep those ghosts hidden.

I nudged his legs as he stared into the forest.

He shook his head sharply. "Yes, of course. I just…"

Smelled a scent he hadn't in thirty years. Thought he never would again. *Happily* thought he never would again. He was sixty-five years old. He'd lived more than half his life as Alpha of the North American Pack. Thirty years as Alpha without so much as an internal ripple of dissension. Thirty years with only a single mutt uprising against us, which we'd quashed and come back stronger than ever.

As Alpha, Jeremy had been adored and respected by his Pack as much as he'd once been adored and respected by only Clay. He'd been an Alpha whose record I couldn't hope to match. I could only try not to totally fuck up what he'd done.

Jeremy had a family, too. Clay and me and the twins, plus a girlfriend who still worshipped the ground he walked on after seven years together. He had an art career so successful none of us had to work if we didn't want to. In short, Jeremy had a damned near perfect life. He certainly seemed to think so. And yet, all it took was one whiff of a scent in a forest, and when I looked at him, I didn't see my Alpha, my friend, the closest thing to a father I had. I saw a boy, wide-eyed and frozen in terror, not knowing which way to run, to hide, to escape.

I let out a warning bark for Clay. Jeremy spun as if to tell me to be quiet. Then he realized what I was doing and nodded. "Yes. Tell him."

I barked again. It was somewhere between, "Stay away," and, "Here I am," which meant, "Keep coming but be careful." He replied with a snarling bark. "I hear you," and his galloping footfalls slowed. I snapped at Jeremy and waved my muzzle toward the cottage. When he didn't move, I lunged at him, trying to drive him back.

"Elena..."

Jeremy's voice was low now, more himself, deep with warning, telling me not to treat him like a defenseless child. I snarled and sniffed the air, trying to find the scent. It was gone now, having been no more than a wisp on the breeze. But that didn't mean Malcolm wasn't out there, taunting us with whiffs of scent.

I looked at the cabin. Kate's trail went to that door. Meaning she could be in there, and if she was, then she was safe, because Malcolm was out here. Was it possible he had a partner? Yes, but unlikely. Very unlikely.

I made a show of snuffling at the rear door. Then I shook my head. It took a moment for Jeremy to rouse from his shock enough to get it.

"You think Kate might be in there," he said. "And we know Malcolm's out *here*."

He didn't wait for me to agree, just strode to the back door and turned the handle. It opened without him needing to snap the lock. I nudged him inside and motioned for him to search. As much as I wanted to do that myself, Clay was coming. I had to tell him about Kate and warn him about Malcolm.

I could see the gold of Clay's fur as he loped through the forest. I forced myself to stay where I was, at the open door, guarding it and listening for any hint of trouble inside. Clay leaped over a bush. Then he skidded to a halt. He lifted his nose and sampled the air. A snort, clearing his nostrils. Another inhalation, so deep I could hear it.

A growl, slow and deep, as if more instinct than intention. His fur rose, and he kept sniffing. Picking up traces of Malcolm's scent, but not enough to be absolutely certain. When I huffed, he broke out of his trance, and he shot toward me so fast I braced for impact. He stopped short and snarled. His fur was on end, tail raised, head down, ears flattened. Blue eyes blazing as he snarled. *If that's who I think it is, what the hell are you doing out here? Is Jeremy in that house? Why aren't you with him?*

I snarled back at that as we faced off, tension snapping between us. Clay lunged to drive me into the house. I grabbed the ruff of his neck and forced his head to the ground. He huffed in surprise. Facing off and snarling at each other was no different than driving me into the safety of the house. Not aggression or true anger. Just communication in a tense situation. Like raising our voices. Grabbing him and forcing his head down was like taking a swing.

I forced his muzzle to the ground. He inhaled, and his body convulsed as he picked up Kate's scent. He let out a sound, half yelp, half whine. I released him, but he kept his nose to the ground, kept sniffing, just as I had, sniffing so hard he snorted dirt and huffed and sneezed, covering the entire area until he was satisfied it was our little girl. Then he pressed his nose against my neck, his breath rippling through my fur while his flanks heaved, as if he was breathing again after twelve hours of holding his breath. We rubbed against each other, eyes closed, hearts still racing.

We found her. We finally found her.

And then Clay remembered that scent on the breeze. He leaped back, muzzle shooting up, nostrils flaring as he struggled to catch it, and I knew he was telling himself he'd been mistaken. Exhausted and panicked over Kate, he'd mistaken Jeremy's scent for his father's. I snorted to get his attention. When that failed, I grabbed his ear. He looked over then, and I nodded. Sniffed. Nodded. *Yes, you smelled exactly who you thought you did.*

His head shot up, eyes widening with, "Oh fuck," as clearly as if he'd spoken the words. He head butted me toward the cabin, and this time I didn't even raise the token protest of a growl. I ran inside.

Clay backed in after me. I growled then, a soft one, to get his attention. I jerked my head toward the door, telling him to stand watch, and there was a second where he hesitated, and I thought, for the first time since I'd become Alpha, he might ignore a direct order.

This was where the two sides of our lives intersected. Where personal and Pack crossed. The beta who should stand guard versus the father desperate to find his daughter.

It lasted only a split second before he chuffed and nodded. But I still walked over, pressing my nose against him, telling him I understood, and I apologized for making him stand behind. In return, he nipped my shoulder. *No apology needed—now go find her.*

A great plan, except Kate wasn't there. I got as far as the main room before Jeremy came from one of the bedrooms and told me as much.

"She came in and walked around, and then she must have left again."

I double-checked. He expected that, perching on the ratty couch and continuing to talk, as much for my benefit as for Clay at the door, keeping him informed.

According to Jeremy's monologue—and confirmed by her trail—she'd come in and gone to the kitchen first. One trail only went in the door, as if she'd looked around. Another rounded the room, as if she'd come back and looked for food, maybe found some. She'd gone through the other rooms, too, but all those trails seemed no more than stepping in and out again. Not taking refuge. Looking for something.

"A phone, I think," Jeremy said as if I'd asked the question. "There's no phone."

He was right. She'd come in, searched for a telephone, and when she didn't find one, took food from the kitchen and headed back out—

Shit!

I raced to the back door and barreled past Clay.

She'd left. Meaning she was outside. Where we'd smelled Malcolm. ⌒

Eleven

KATE'S TRAIL VANISHED several times. She walked through another stream. Then she climbed another tree. Hiding her scent.

Still, I could figure out her trajectory and, between the three of us, we grabbed her new trail quickly enough. We lost Malcolm's scent, too. His stayed gone, though, and we never were able to pick it up on the ground. Did that mean he hadn't pursued Kate? Or, as I'd considered earlier, was he wearing the carbon-lined jumpsuit and only letting us catch a whiff now and then, toying with us? Maybe, but if he was on Kate's trail, I should have picked up the occasional faint scent of him. Or so I told myself as I covered mile after mile through the dark forest.

Clay and I ran side by side. We crossed streams and tore up hills and bounded over rocks and startled enough wildlife to feed the Pack for a week. We even passed a yipping coyote, his fur on end, snarling as he backed away, ready to flee the moment we took any interest in him. When we kept going, he howled his triumph to the moon. I'm sure it would be a story to tell his grand-pups—the day he'd scared two massive wolves off his territory.

Jeremy stayed in human form, jogging, more or less keeping pace, mainly because we bobbed and weaved along Kate's trail, which went everywhere, and he could plot our trajectory and catch up.

Jeremy had contacted the others, warning them about Malcolm and telling them about Kate. In other words, it was a much more eloquent version of my barking to Clay earlier. *Come here, but approach with caution.* Of course, the fact we were on the move meant they hadn't reached us yet.

When I first caught the scent, I thought I was wrong. I'd been following Kate's trail too long, my nose stuffed with her smell. I'd raised my head to peer into the night—and keep me from plowing into trees—and I still smelled her. On the breeze, not the ground. I didn't dare believe it until I heard Clay chuff beside me and, with a sudden bound, he passed me, the beta gone, the father taking over, racing ahead.

I caught up in a few long strides. We hit a downed tree, one that had fallen long ago, brambles growing up around it, a perfect hiding place for forest animals. Or for a lost little girl. Clay poked his head in one spot. I found another and—

"Mommy!"

Kate flew at me, arms wrapping around my neck, face burying in the ruff at my neck. Her whole body pressed against me, shaking, as she sobbed, the first time I'd heard her cry in years. Body-wracking sobs, her arms wrapped so tight I had to sip breaths. Clay pressed in beside me, reaching as far as he could, snuffling at her, searching for injury.

"Daddy!"

I backed out, ceding my spot as her arms went around his neck, face in his fur, sobbing and telling him she was sorry, so sorry.

I hopped over the log and Changed. By the time I finished, Jeremy was there, murmuring, "Your clothing is on the log," as I panted, catching my breath. I pulled it on. It had taken close to ten minutes to Change forms, but Clay and Kate were where I'd left them, Kate still clinging to him, still crying, softer now, approaching exhaustion by the hitches in her voice. When Clay heard me, he nudged her and backed out of the tree fall. Kate let go and stumbled out beside him. I was crouched there, waiting. She threw herself into my arms and started crying again. Clay sniffed and prodded her, again searching for any sign of injury.

"I'm fine, Dad," she said, reaching back for him.

The kids had known what we were since they were four. That hadn't been my plan. I'd wanted to wait until they were nearing their teens. Clay had disagreed, and I'd come to realize he had a point. Now I knew he'd been absolutely right. Knowing what we were not only kept them safer and immersed them completely in Pack life, but immersed them fully in our lives too. To them, we were Mom and Dad, as wolf or human, their comfort with the dichotomy something I hadn't achieved until I'd been a werewolf longer than they'd been alive.

Clay sniffed Kate again. Then he looked up at me, blue eyes clouded with worry. There was no smell of blood. Nothing more than dirt and scratches and tears, but something...

"Is she all right?" Jeremy asked, staying where he was, giving us our moment.

I hesitated before I said, "She is," because something wasn't right, and like Clay, I didn't know what it was. No cuts or broken bones or other physical trauma, but there was a note in her crying, something beyond the simple fear of a lost child, something almost broken.

I looked at Clay again. He huffed, saying we'd talk later, figure it out later. For now, having heard Jeremy's voice, Kate was pulling back from me, turning to him. He came over and caught her up in an embrace.

"You're all right?" he whispered.

She nodded, but when he glanced at me, I caught the same look I'd gotten from Clay. *Something's wrong.*

"I'm going to have Jeremy call Uncle Nick," I said. "They'll bring a car as close as they can get, then your dad can carry you to it. I imagine you're tired?"

She nodded. I led her to the fallen tree and we sat on it. I handed her the missing shoe. Then I pulled a granola bar and juice box from my jacket. She took and opened them, her fingers trembling, me reaching over to help. She didn't argue with that. Just let me help. Which told me something was definitely wrong.

"Kate?"

She looked up, blue eyes meeting mine, hers filling with tears. "I'm sorry, Mom. I only wanted to get away. That's all I was doing. But he kept coming after me—"

"Someone was chasing you?"

"Following me. From the cabin. I went out for a walk, and I heard someone in the woods. Between me and the cottage."

I glanced at Jeremy. He motioned for me to stay calm. She was relaying her story, her own tone steadying as she relaxed, safe at last. Having me panic wouldn't help.

"You heard someone," I said. "Did you see him?"

She shook her head. Her night vision is good, and her hearing is excellent. Secondary werewolf characteristics. We had no idea if she would ever become one, but she had inherited that much.

"I could only hear him. I thought maybe it was a hunter or a hiker, so I hid, waiting for him to pass, but he wasn't going anywhere, just kept hanging around, like he was looking or waiting for something. Then I saw him bent over and heard him sniffing, and I knew it was a werewolf, and he'd found my trail."

Clay joined us then, wearing the clothes Jeremy had carried for him. He lifted Kate up and put her on his lap. Whenever he'd done that in the last three years, she'd squirmed off with a roll of her eyes, but now she stayed, leaning against him as more tension slid from her face. She seemed ready to resume her story. Then she rubbed her arms, as if chilled. Clay took off his jacket and wrapped it around her.

"Then what, sweetheart?" he said. "That's when you went in the stream?"

She nodded. "I came up with a plan. I walked in the stream a long ways, as quietly as I could. Then I climbed a tree, and I crawled through a bunch of them before I jumped down onto some rocks. I headed back to the cabin. Or I thought that's where I was going, but I just kept walking and walking, until I knew I'd gone too far and by then it was light and I didn't recognize anything and..."

"You were lost."

She nodded. "I kept walking. A few times, I thought I heard someone, so I hid. I even broke into two cabins, but no one had a phone and no one was around and..." She took a deep breath. "When it got dark, I hid in here."

She seemed to be trembling now, but when Clay shifted, his jacket falling from around her, she was rubbing her arms harder as if...I didn't know what. Obviously she was cold and anxious from the memories, warming and calming herself, but something in the gesture seemed familiar. The connection wouldn't come, though. Jeremy crouched beside the log.

"Can you tell us why you left the cabin, Kate?"

She started shaking almost convulsively, and I shot a glare at Jeremy. We didn't need to do this now. He said, "You aren't in any trouble. We just want to know," and caught another glower for that. I'm not sure what was worse—pushing her for a confession when she was still distraught, or promising she wouldn't be punished for the transgression. Clay looked over too but quizzically. Wondering what the hell Jeremy was doing. He was usually very careful about that, not disciplining the twins nor giving them shelter when we did. When it came to our kids, we were the bosses; he was support staff.

"Kate?" he prodded.

"I...needed to go out. For air."

"In the middle of the night?"

"It was almost five."

"But still dark out."

I rocked forward, ready to squelch this line of questioning, but a look from Clay stopped me. *He's going somewhere. Let him get there.*

Kate nodded.

"You know that you aren't supposed to leave the house without telling someone," he said. "That would go doubly out here, in a strange place, wouldn't it?"

A nod. She'd stopped rubbing her arms but continued trembling, her gaze down. I squirmed and fought the urge to rescue her.

"So to leave the cabin, at night, when it was still dark, without telling anyone where you were going..."

"I wasn't going anywhere," she blurted. "Just on the porch. It was hot. Really hot."

"But you *left* the porch. You must have, if this man got between you and the cabin."

"I... It didn't help. Going out onto the porch. It was still really hot and I..." Tears filled her eyes. "I've been feeling weird."

"Sick?" I asked, alarmed. The twins had had maybe three colds and one bout of the flu in their entire lives.

"No. I just feel...weird. I get mad at things, and I know I shouldn't be so mad, but I just can't help it. Everything seems to be going wrong all at once, and sometimes I can't sleep, and

I just wanted to go out. I knew I shouldn't, and I meant to stay on the porch, and then I only meant to walk into the yard, and then just to the stream, and it seemed okay. I could still see the cabin, and I wasn't going far. I didn't *mean* to go far."

She'd started rubbing her arms again. When I leaned over to take her hand, she jumped, but didn't resist, holding her arm out as I peeled back her sleeve.

"Is your arm bothering you?" I said.

"Just tonight. It feels…weird." A flash of frustration now, more like my little girl. "I don't know how else to say it. Just weird."

Her arm looked fine. I was patting it and getting ready to pull down her sleeve when a muscle twitched. Then another. Faint twitches. Nothing to worry—

A ripple, like something moving under her skin.

"Mom!" Kate's head jerked up, her gaze meeting mine. "What was that?"

"The muscles are twitching," I said. "That's all."

That wasn't all. I knew that wasn't all. But I told myself I was overreacting. And I refused to look up at Clay or over at Jeremy.

I rubbed my hand over her arm, a quick massage, but as I did, I felt a roughness there, and the hairs on my neck prickled. I brushed my finger over her forearm, lighter, and felt nothing, just the soft skin and fine hairs of childhood. I hesitated and

I wanted to pull away, keep saying I'd been wrong. Still over-reacting. Stressed and tired and—

And I knew what I'd seen. What I'd felt.

I rubbed my thumb over the bottom of her arm. A slight rasp, like Clay's cheek hours after shaving, no beard shadow to be seen, yet the hairs there, infinitesimally small but undeniably present. The very tips of hair waiting to push through. ⌒

Twelve

OM?" KATE'S VOICE was high, that anxiety from earlier lingering, ready to reignite at the first sign of trouble.

Tension strummed beneath the surface, erupting in anger at home, her temper shorter than ever. Out here, though, that same tension took another form after her terrifying day in the forest. Emotions running close to the surface.

"Hormones," Logan had said.

Yes. Hormones. A sure sign of puberty in another child, an older child. But in ours? A sign of something else.

I took a deep breath.

"Mom?"

Clay's arms tightened around her, and he rubbed her arms, not checking for anything because he already knew, had known the moment he saw muscles moving under her skin.

Just comforting her now, massaging her arms and murmuring, "It's okay. Everyone's tired. We're just glad we found you. So glad we found you."

He hugged her tighter, but she wriggled out, my old Kate coming back, pushing to her feet and turning to eye us.

"What is it?" she said.

"Noth—" I began, but Clay shook his head. She wasn't a baby. She couldn't be placated with empty reassurances.

I looked at her. "Can we talk about this later? Uncle Nick's coming—"

"He isn't here yet," she said. "I want to know."

I cleared my throat. "I would rather wait. Like your dad said, we're all tired, and there are a few things we need to..."

I trailed off. I was going to say there were things we needed to check, to be sure before we said anything, but that was a lie. There was nothing to check. No way of knowing if what I feared was happening except the seemingly incontrovertible proof that it was.

"I've got this." Clay caught Kate by the shirt hem. She resisted, but he tugged her onto his knee and held her there when she squirmed. "What do you think it is, sweetheart?"

She shrugged, but there was enough hesitation in it to tell me he'd hit the bulls-eye.

"You have an idea," he said. "The best we can do is tell you you're wrong."

She looked up at him. "Or the worst."

He nodded. "Or the worst."

And there it was. If my greatest fear was the loss of my children or my mate, this was the second greatest. The part of me that wanted a normal life for them. I call it the human part; Clay calls it the mother part. I want my children to have the easiest and best possible life, and I'm torn, because I don't know what that is. Life as a werewolf? Or life as a human?

Other supernaturals can joke about the benefits of being a werewolf: prolonged life, improved health, super strength, enhanced senses, high metabolism. "Where do I sign up?" But the truth is that very, very few of them ever try to "sign up"— to get bitten by a werewolf—because they know they don't really want that. A prolonged lifespan doesn't help when most of us don't live past fifty. It's a short, brutal life. A life spent enduring the torture rack of changing to a wolf every week. A life spent fighting and managing our worst impulses, our most violent ones, the ones that see a running human and, for just an instant, think "dinner."

But for my children, it's more than that. This is their birthright. It's the life they've grown up in. They see that— despite all the disadvantages—we are happy. Their parents are madly in love. Their family is stable and healthy. They have an extended network of uncles and cousins. And they are the center of that world, as pups are in any pack. So they expect to grow up and join that pack. To become a true part of it. To be werewolves. And if they can't? Therein lies that second-greatest fear. Not that my children won't Change, but that the disappointment of not Changing will crush them, and we'll be forced to make a hellish decision. To insist they live as humans. Or to turn them into werewolves.

"What do you think is happening?" Clay said.

"That I'm Changing. I'm becoming a werewolf." She squirmed in his arms, not trying to get free now, just squirming, her gaze darting about, and I knew what she was looking for. Her brother. She wanted him here to explain for her. To put her hopes and fears into words so she didn't have to say them, didn't have to admit them.

"But I can't be," she said. "I'm too young, and I know what you and Mom say, that it might never happen for us, or that it might for Logan, but not for me, because you're both bitten and I'm a girl and... And either way, I'm too young. I know you were young, Dad, but that was different because you got bitten and that definitely hasn't happened to me, and if I was a hereditary werewolf, nothing would happen until I was at least fifteen and..." She gulped air, slowing herself down, gaze lowered. "I'm afraid I'm..." She struggled for a word. "Misinterpreting. That's what Lo would say. I'm misinterpreting the data because I want..." She sucked in breath. "I want it so bad and I know…" Her gaze lifted to mine. "I'm sorry, Mom. I know you don't like me to say that—"

"I've never said—"

"But I know." A twist of a smile. "How many times have you told us it might not happen? That it probably won't."

"I just don't want…" *To get your hopes up.* But I couldn't bring myself to say that. It implied that this was something desirable, and with that, I knew she was right. However hard I'd tried to be neutral on the subject, my bias came through.

"It's not that I don't want you to be a werewolf, baby," I said slowly. "It's that I don't want you—"

"—to want it. You don't want us to be disappointed." She wriggled from Clay's lap and moved beside me, her hand sliding into mine. "I'm going to be disappointed if it doesn't happen, and you know that, and you don't want me to be."

I took a moment to find my voice. "So you're worried that these symptoms are in your imagination."

She nodded.

"They aren't. The mood swings are part of it. The overheating, mild fever, especially at night. The need to get outside, to move, to work it off. The restlessness and going out at night are signs you could probably predict, but the rest of it isn't anything we've discussed. Nothing we planned to discuss for a few years, until you might be old enough to experience it."

I paused, pushing down the voice in my head that screamed, *She's only eight! Eight!*

I took her arm and ran my hand over it. The muscles had stopped twitching, the tiny coarse hairs receding. "That's what happens. If we go too long without Changing. The muscles twitching like that. And there was...I could feel hair..."

"Fur."

"Right."

I expected Clay to cut in, stop my fumbling and take over again, but he didn't move. Kate's attention was on me, completely on me. Relying on me.

I took a deep breath. "If—when—it happens again, if you rub your bare arm, you'll feel it. That doesn't mean you're Changing or that you'll Change anytime soon. It might not even mean that you'll ever—"

"I get it, Mom. No guarantees. I don't need the fine print."

She sounded like her dad then. No, let's be honest, she sounded like me. Impatience mingled with sarcasm.

"Okay, well, presuming it means you'll Change, this is just the first stage. It'll probably be months. It could even be years. Your dad and I don't have any personal experience with that— the progression for hereditary werewolves. Noah went through it last, obviously, so I'll have you talk to him. And Reese."

I added Reese, knowing that would be Kate's preference. With Noah, it was more of your typical teenage cousin situation, where they got along fine, but didn't interact much one-on-one. Reese had been an only child; Noah had half-siblings, and the fact that he had no interest in contacting them said a lot about that relationship. They'd been the children of his stepfather, who'd made it very clear he didn't appreciate having to support another man's kid. I suspect there'd been a strain between the children, and so playing big brother wasn't a role that would ever come naturally to Noah.

The rumble of a car engine sounded in the distance.

"That's our ride," Clay said. "We should start walking and meet him. You want a piggyback, Kate?"

She looked at him. "Um, no. I'm nine, Dad."

"Not for another month. Still time left. You should take advantage of it."

She sighed, rolled her eyes and fell in step beside me. He darted up behind her, grabbed her and swung her onto his shoulders.

"Fine," she grumbled. "I'll humor you. Just don't let anyone else see."

"Oh, I'm gonna make sure they see. And take pictures."

She sighed, folded her arms on top of his head and leaned forward, eyes closing, enjoying the ride, perhaps for the last time. ⌒

Thirteen

ICK MET US halfway. He swung Kate down off her father's shoulders. Yes, she'd allowed herself to be seen, but only because Uncle Nick didn't count. He gave her a fierce hug. She told him he stunk of sweat. We all did, but only Nick would care, so he was the one she had to needle.

"You want to walk back?" he said. "Because I'm pretty sure if I smell, the truck does, too."

"Nah, *you* can walk." She went on ahead, still talking. "Looks like you could use it. You've put on a few pounds."

Nick shot a glance down toward his perfectly flat stomach.

"Made you look," she said, without turning. Then she spun around, walking backward. "How's Vanessa? She still putting up with you?"

"If she wasn't, then I'd have canceled taking you and Logan to Boston next weekend, wouldn't I? Now that I think about it, though, maybe I should make it a guy weekend. Just take your brother."

"He won't go without me."

"Oh, I bet I could convince him."

She shook her head and continued walking. Jeremy strode up beside her. I fell back with Clay and Nick.

"Nice to see she's bounced back," Nick said. "I swear, every time I see her, I feel more like I'm talking to you."

"Me?" I said.

"That's who I'm looking at. Your smart mouth and his"—a chin jerk at Clay—"cockiness. I pity the guy who falls for her."

"Which will be in the distant, distant future," Clay said. "Or you'll have more reason than that to pity him."

They bantered as I waited until I was certain that if Kate was still within earshot, she wasn't paying attention to us.

"She didn't take off," I cut in. "Kate, I mean. She had a reason for leaving the cabin."

"'Course she did," Nick said.

I looked at him.

"I knew she didn't just take off," he said. "Sure, she's been bratty lately, but she's not going to give you guys a heart attack for kicks. I kept my mouth shut, because if I said she wouldn't leave without a reason, you'd both hear, 'She's been kidnapped,' which wouldn't have helped matters. So what happened?"

I told him.

"Shit," he said when I finished. "You really think...?" He caught my look. "Poor kid." A few steps in silence, then, "Okay, that's not what anyone wants for her at this age, but you've got to remember a few things. One, she's tough. Two, it might not happen for years. Three, if it does happen sooner... It might not be the worst thing ever." When I gave him a look, he lifted his hands in defense. "I'm just suggesting that whatever Clay's faults—"

"I'm right beside you," Clay said.

"Which means I'm not talking about you behind your back. A friend wouldn't do that. Whatever Clay's faults, Changing at an early age didn't do too much damage. Unlike Clay, Kate has been properly socialized."

"I'm still beside you."

"I still don't care. Kate has everything she needs to get through this, and if you want to find a silver lining, just think that you won't need to worry about the Change and puberty hitting at the same time. If it's like Clay's case, she'll find the Changes easier and the life easier. She'll just skip the drawbacks that made him what he is."

Clay's foot shot out to trip Nick, who circled to get to my other side, and continued, "If Kate's Changing already, we'll deal with it. The bigger problem right now is the guy who drove her into the forest."

I hadn't exactly forgotten that, but I'd shoved it aside. I analyzed the data again, turning it over in my much more level frame of mind.

"Maybe we were wrong." I caught their looks. "Okay, I'm grasping at straws. Like Jeremy told you on the phone, we smelled Malcolm. Three of us, independently, meaning there's no mistake. But I checked his transmitter on the drive here, and he was still in Bulgaria."

"His *transmitter* was," Clay said. "We've been waiting for him to realize he's bugged and cut the damn thing out. We hoped he'd damage it if he did. Or smash it. Unfortunately, he's not that stupid. He removed it carefully and left it behind."

"But the signal has been moving," I said. "It's stayed within a hundred-mile radius in the last week, but it's moving."

"Yeah, because if it stops moving, we'd know he's found it. He's probably inserted it in some innocent Bulgarian or stuck it on the back of a truck. Fact is, he's here, and we need to figure out what the hell we're going to do about it."

"Kill him?" Nick said.

Clay glanced over.

Nick gave a rueful smile. "Yes, I know, we've been trying for three years now. I'm the only one who's even gotten close enough to give it a shot. Which I blew."

"No," I said. "We all had a shot, Clay and I in Los Angeles, you in Detroit. At least you sent him running. We didn't even manage that."

"We will this time, darling," Clay said. "Malcolm's next stop is a shallow grave."

*

To GET TO where Kate had holed up, Nick had needed to circle the forest and come down a logging road. Which meant that it was faster to walk the few miles back to our cabin. Clay and I decided to do that. If Malcolm was around, it was always possible we'd catch his scent.

That, though, was only our excuse for the trek. A poor one, given that if he smelled Clay and me together, he sure as hell wasn't coming near us. Malcolm was in his eighties. Not a frail old man by any means, unfortunately. The Nasts had been experimenting on cryogenics with him. I have no idea how long they'd been doing it or how successfully—they were admitting nothing—but I'd peg him at closer to Jeremy and Antonio's physical age, likely a combination of the experiments and a lifetime spent in top condition. In other words, in human terms, he was the equivalent of a forty-eight-year-old athlete.

Still, that didn't make him a match for Clay. I'd bested him myself in Los Angeles. He'd escaped death then only because gun-toting Cabal goons had insisted on it. If Malcolm scented the two of us in the forest, he'd keep his head down until he got us separated.

The real reason we walked together? So we could talk about Kate. Hashing it out. Clay knew my fears went well beyond timing. My own Change had been horrific. The fact that Clay bit me without my permission? Yes, he'd done it on impulse, in a fog of panic. No, he'd never entertained the possibility I wouldn't survive. Yes, he'd regretted that bite as he'd regretted nothing else in his life. But all that didn't change the fact of what he'd done and what I'd suffered, and it had taken me ten years to forgive him. It doesn't matter if I can honestly say now that, if he'd given me the option, I'd go through that hell again to become what I am today, to have the life I have today. Even the thought that one of my children might someday ask to be bitten had always been enough to send me into a maelstrom of memories and nightmares.

But here it was, and we had no choice. I knew what could happen. Not everyone survived the first Change. Nick was right—Kate was strong and she had the best support system possible. Jeremy got me through my Change; he could do the same for Kate. But my children were already anomalies, displaying secondary characteristics so young.

What if…God help me. What if they *couldn't* Change. If their bodies could not physically complete the process?

There were many what-ifs. Many nightmares. And even to let my brain approach one of them sent it spiraling toward madness.

That's why Clay insisted we walk. To talk me through it as only he could. To remind me that werewolves were not aberrations of nature. They were a species. A species that bears all the hallmarks of a healthy and successful one, including the ability to reproduce. We'd had the same talks when I was pregnant, when I'd wake racked by nightmares of my babies Changing inside me, of giving birth to deformed half-wolf infants who would not survive. Groundless fears. Nature had provided then, and so she would again. I had to believe that.

As we were walking, my phone buzzed with an incoming text from a number I didn't recognize.

Have you found your little girl?

I tensed. Clay read it over my shoulder and swore.

"Do I reply?" I said.

Before he could answer, another text came in.

She's a cutie, but a little young for me.

I texted back. *Maybe I'm more your style. Let's meet and find out.*

When he answered, I swore I heard Malcolm's low chuckle. *No, you are definitely not my style, Elena. Too many complications. And I don't really have time for that anyway. I have a different goal in mind. Reminding you and Clayton why I am not a man to be trifled with.*

We're not trifling, I replied. *We're serious. Dead serious. Come out of the shadows and find out.*

Do you know the secret to my success, Elena? I have exactly the right amount of confidence. I know when I can take on a wolf and when I should await a better opportunity. You and your mate together are a little more than I care to tangle with. I've had a long night. I'm looking for an easy challenge. I think I've found it, too.

I glanced at Clay, hoping he'd supply the clever retort I couldn't manage as my heart picked up speed.

Clay took the phone and typed: *Okay, I'll bite.*

I'm sure you will, given the opportunity. Is Clayton there?

Clay typed back, *Yeah.*

A direct reply. Even better. I'm wondering, Clayton, if you're getting complacent in that adorably domestic life of yours. Losing your edge?

Come see me and find out, Clay replied.

Perhaps not your physical edge, but your mental one? That sharp mind of yours dulling with inactivity? Because I'm surprised at you, out there chasing that little girl of yours. What interest does a proper wolf have in a little girl?

I have a great deal of interest in my daughter, which you will discover if you ever come near her again.

Oh, I don't doubt it. But let me repeat the question: what interest does a proper wolf have in a little girl?

Clay read that and breathed, "Logan."

"What?" I said.

"He doesn't mean me. He means himself. That *he* has no interest in—"

Another text. *I'm going to leave you and your lovely mate alone tonight, Clayton. I have a date with another blond, I fear. A young wolf I saw wandering about with a little boy. Hard to believe you'd leave your only son with a boy little more than a child himself.*

We broke into a run before we'd even finished reading the message. ⌒

Fourteen

LOGAN. OH, SHIT. *Logan.*

Goddamn it, Malcolm was right. We should have seen this coming. To him, women were only good for sex and breeding. Even I wasn't more than a freak of nature. Sons were what counted. If Malcolm wanted to hurt Clay, he wouldn't go after our daughter.

As Clay talked to Jeremy, I called Reese. After four rings, it went to his voice mail. I left a message and then texted, telling him to call me right away.

"It's past midnight," Clay said when I told him. "He's just asleep. Keep dialing. Jeremy's contacting the others, seeing who's closest."

We were, as it turned out. By the time Jeremy phoned back, we could see the lights of the cabin. I tried to break into a sprint, but Clay grabbed my arm and held me back. In other words: don't go running pell-mell toward the cabin, because we might be walking into a trap.

We slowed to a fast walk. When I did, I called Reese again. I could hear his phone ringing inside the cabin.

"He's not sleeping through that," I said. "Not after five calls. Not both him and Logan."

"I know," Clay said grimly.

We looped around until we could see the front porch. The front door stood open. I rocked forward, ready to run, but stopped myself before Clay had to.

"Cover me," he said.

I nodded. He proceeded toward the door. I walked backwards behind him, peering into the night, listening and, most of all, sniffing, making sure no one snuck up while his attention was focused on that open door.

We reached it without incident. Everything was silent, inside and out. I crouched at the porch but picked up no scent. I was about to say so when I caught one in the air. I followed it to the front window.

It was a light scent, there on the sill, as if the intruder had his gloves off and touched it when he peered inside. And I say "intruder" not "Malcolm" because it wasn't his scent. I motioned Clay over. He sniffed the spot and shook his head. No one he knew. Definitely werewolf, though. I'd been wrong.

Malcolm had someone with him. Not a partner, but flunkies. Wolves willing to do his bidding. Foreign wolves, if neither Clay nor I recognized their scent.

The Bulgarian Pack. They'd insisted they weren't sheltering him. They just didn't want us on their land looking for him. We'd always wondered if they were lying. Now I was sure of it. Malcolm had recruited a few to help him clear the way for his return.

As we returned to the front door, Karl drove up. Hope got out first. I left Clay in the open doorway and jogged over.

Before I could say a word, Hope reach up and wrapped her arms around me. I embraced her back and said, "Thanks for coming."

"Of course." She squeezed my arm. "It'll be okay. Malcolm's not stupid enough to hurt them."

And that was, perhaps, the most sensible and reassuring thing anyone had said so far. Malcolm was a psychotic son of a bitch, but he knew if he hurt one of our children, we'd hunt him to the ends of the earth.

"What's happening?" Karl said.

"We just got back," I said as we started for the cabin. "We haven't gone in yet."

"The door was open?"

I nodded. "There's a scent I don't recognize by the window. Werewolf, though. All's quiet inside. Reese's phone is in there but…" I inhaled sharply. "He's not answering." I asked Hope, "Have you picked up anything?"

"No. Which doesn't mean much these days."

"And if the trade was offered again, I'd take it in a second," Karl said.

Hope made a noise in her throat. She disagreed. I didn't. As the daughter of Lucifer, Hope had inherited her father's sixth sense for trouble. She could hear chaotic thoughts and catch visions of chaos, mostly negative and mostly violent. Which would be difficult enough except, to her, that chaos used to be like fine wine. She'd craved it, even as it had ripped holes in her psyche. After having Nita she'd lost that hunger. Which meant she lost some of her power, and that's what she regretted. But like Karl, I was glad of it, even if it meant her powers weren't as keen as they'd once been.

We reached the cabin.

"Karl, I want you outside," I whispered. "Hope, can you stay here at the door?"

As the mate of a Pack wolf and mother of his child, Hope considered herself Pack and had made it clear that orders were fine, but I framed it as request.

"Of course," she said, and we left her there, with Karl moving into the yard to stand watch as Clay and I slipped into the cabin.

"No smells," Clay whispered in my ear. "I was checking while you were gone."

I was about to say that of course there were no scents—we knew the intruders were covering theirs. But he'd said "smell" not "scent." It meant he didn't smell blood. We'd both been thinking of that even if we'd never voiced the fear.

The main room and kitchen were clear. The bedroom doors were open with no sign of anyone in the rooms. The only closed door—

"Mom?" Logan's voice came through that door—the bathroom one. "Is that you?"

"Logan?"

The closed door opened and Reese peeked out. "Clear?"

Clay pushed open the door, shoving him back.

"Hey!" Reese said. "I was checking, okay?"

Clay muttered something that could be an apology. He reached to scoop Logan up, but our son raised his hands, fending him off, then leaning in for an awkward hug.

"Hey, Dad. Is Kate all right?"

"She's fine. They're on their way. Are you—?"

"I'm fine." He smiled at me. "Hey, Momma."

A hug for me, too, not Kate's crushing embrace—our son wasn't a hugger. I'd been the last to fall off his list, and I still missed it, but I respected his personal space. I understood it, too. Outside the Pack, I stiffen to a mannequin if someone tries to hug me. Clay won't even shake hands. So our kid comes by it naturally.

Clay was on the other side of the door, inspecting it. I glanced over to see a dent nearly busted through to a hole. The knob was bent. Someone had been trying to break in.

"In Reese's truck," I said. "Everyone. Now." ⌒

Fifteen

CLAY DROVE. KARL and Hope followed in Karl's Lexus. I texted the others to meet us at the highway. We'd return for our things later. For all we knew, Malcolm had brought the whole damned Bulgarian Pack. In that cabin, we'd be sitting ducks.

Which is exactly what Reese and Logan had been, as Reese explained what had happened. When Reese heard someone skulking around the cabin he'd grabbed Logan and retreated to the bathroom. Only after they got in there had he realized his phone was still in the bedroom. Before he could go back for it the intruders had walked in the front door.

"Two of them," Reese said. "They didn't talk, but I could hear two sets of footsteps—one boots, the other shoes. They figured out where we were and tried the door. I'd brought a chair from the dining room and wedged it under. I knew that wouldn't hold very long, but they didn't seem to try very hard. They broke the handle. They bashed the door. I had a shard of the mirror, and was waiting for a hand to come through that door. It never did. After a few moments they left."

"Did you say anything to them?"

"Hell, no. If they heard my accent, they'd know who it was, and I'd much rather they thought it was Clay waiting on the other side of that door."

"So you don't know why they left?"

"They never said a word."

"Did they seem to search for anything in the cabin?"

"No, just us."

Which they could have gotten to, if they'd tried harder. Maybe when it turned out to be more than a simple matter of grabbing Logan in his bed, they feared we'd show up at any second. Or maybe it was exactly what Hope said: Malcolm was being an asshole, nothing more and nothing less. Yet Malcolm wasn't a typical bully, content to huff and puff and watch his victims scurry like frightened little piggies. He had a plan; he just hadn't launched it yet.

We pulled into the parking lot of a business long closed for the night. It was empty and it was open ground, which meant we could circle the wagons and watch for trouble as we talked. We did so literally, cars and trucks in the middle, kids left sleeping in Jeremy's SUV, the younger guys on guard duty while the rest of us talked.

I got everyone up to speed as quickly as I could. Then Jeremy and I walked away from the group to discuss the situation.

"We need to split up," I said. "You and Antonio take the kids and Noah. Get someplace safe. The rest of us will go after Malcolm."

"And how will you find him?"

"He can't walk around in public in a jumpsuit. He's going to need to ditch that and resort to the spray, which I can track."

"All right. So you'll track him by scent. Starting where?" Jeremy gave a meaningful look around us.

"He won't go far. He has a plan."

"I'm sure he does. I'm equally sure that plan doesn't mean going after you or Clayton. His targets are those he can threaten and possibly hurt, and in return, hurt Clay and hurt me, and perhaps even hurt you, because he does not appreciate being hunted by a woman."

"Yes, but—"

"No buts. Malcolm has three primary targets. Logan, Kate and me. In that order. You are correct that he isn't stupid enough to kill the children. But he is not above kidnapping them. What you saw tonight was a cat toying with mice.

Batting them about to get our attention. Now, when he strikes, we'll suffer doubly because we knew it was coming and were powerless to stop it."

"Which is why I'm getting the kids and you—"

"To safety? If you hide the mice, the cat will follow. You can't simply remove us from the playing field."

"I sure as hell can try."

"You can. Effectively even. Ask Benicio to take us in. Put us in Cortez Cabal headquarters, surrounded by armed guards. Malcolm isn't a genie. He can't pop in and attack us. So, yes, you can safely stow us while you hunt for him. But should you?"

"Is that really a question?"

He stopped in front of me. "It is absolutely a question, Elena. Once Malcolm realizes we are safe, he'll retreat and you will not find him for months. Do you expect the children and me to live in Cabal custody for months?"

"Of course not."

We resumed walking. A noise behind me made me turn. Clay had thumped down onto the hood of Karl's Lexus a little too hard, which could mean he was amusing himself, jerking Karl's chain, but I knew that thump was for my benefit. Telling me we'd gone far enough out of his range.

We crossed the road and slowly circled back.

"I don't like what you're suggesting."

"I don't believe I made a suggestion," Jeremy said.

"I won't use my kids as bait."

"Then use me."

"He'll see through that one. Like you said, you're at the bottom of the target list. No offense."

"I have been at the bottom of my father's list for my entire life, Elena. The only reason I'm a target is because my death would teach Clay a lesson. One Malcolm has wanted to impart for forty years. Punish Clay for choosing me. Show him I'm easily removed from the equation and therefore was never worthy of his attention. But if he comes after me, someone might think he cares about me. It's a complication that moves me to the bottom of the list."

"Meaning if the kids disappear, he'll follow them. The best bait is the twins, with you as guardian. If it's just the three of you, though, that's an obvious trap. I'd need to send Antonio as a guard, and probably a couple of the boys."

"I would suggest Noah and Reese. Noah because he's too young still to help you. Reese will keep the twins amused, and he's already proven he's a good guard."

"I'll just need to make sure he realizes I'm sending him away because I trust him with my kids, not because I think he makes a better babysitter than a fighter."

"Yes."

"What about Karl? Or Nick?"

"Karl's a first-rate fighter, with a known grudge against Malcolm. Leaving him with us will make Malcolm think twice. As for Nick, he's better with you. Give us Hope."

"If Karl will let me."

A hard look. No words, just that look.

I sighed. "I know, it's not up to Karl. Tell him. Be Alpha. It's just harder when I'm asking him to put his *wife* in danger."

"No, she'll be safer with us *and* more useful with us. Also Malcolm won't question why she's in our camp. Women and children taking refuge."

After a few steps, I said, "I need to try it my way first."

"I know. Tell me what you have in mind."

*

THE KIDS WERE asleep in Jeremy's SUV, which Clay had borrowed for the trip. Jeremy had driven up in my car. There were many concessions Clay and I were willing to make for our children. Owning an SUV—or, worse, a minivan—wasn't one of them. Jeremy took that responsibility, though he had managed to convince me to upgrade to a luxury sedan "for the safety features." And if I was kind of happy to chuck my old beater for heated leather seats, I'll never admit it out loud.

I climbed into the back of the SUV, where the kids were sound asleep. When I kissed Kate's cheek, her eyelids fluttered open.

"I need you to go with Jeremy tonight."

She nodded sleepily.

"Antonio, Reese, Noah and Hope will be with you."

"Logan, too?" she murmured.

Her brother tossed in his sleep, as if hearing his name, but too tired to wake.

"Of course."

She wrapped her arms around my neck. "I'll be okay, Mom."

"I know. But if you have any symptoms, call and we'll talk."

"Jeremy can handle them. He's the medic."

"I don't mean medically. Just to talk."

Another hug. Tighter. "I'll be fine. Now that I know what's happening, I won't be such a bitch."

I gave her a stern look.

"What?" A ghost of her father's smile. "That's the right word, isn't it? For a female wolf?"

I laughed softly and kissed her forehead. Then I stretched over Kate and kissed Logan's cheek. He kept his eyes closed, but mumbled, "'Night, Momma."

"'Night, baby," I said and closed the door. ⌒

Sixteen

OUR "WOMEN AND children" group had left in Jeremy's SUV. Everyone not driving would take a window and watch for tails. This was stage one of my plan. Get them into a hotel—a big anonymous one in a big anonymous city, which meant leaving Vermont.

For the first hour, we took an alternate route, but stayed close enough that a call would bring us in minutes. We'd seen no sign of pursuers since leaving the cabin, though, and no suspicious vehicles appeared now.

We met up at the hotel. Jeremy and I took the kids inside. Antonio kept the SUV and headed in the direction of home with Nick, Morgan, Reese and Noah.

Hope and Karl scouted outside. After a few minutes, they came in...and Clay and I snuck Jeremy, Hope and the kids out the back door. We bustled them into the SUV, which

Antonio had circled around to a back road. Then he drove off with Jeremy, Hope and the twins hidden in the back—leaving Nick and Morgan behind.

That was our scenario. If Malcolm and his mutts managed to keep up, they'd think all their targets were in one place for the night. My hope was that, with his own "Pack" to support him, Malcolm would attempt an attack...while Jeremy and the twins were sixty miles away in another hotel.

We took two rooms, Clay and I in one, with Nick, Morgan and Karl in the adjoining suite. We didn't even say goodnight. Just got our keys and retreated.

It was almost four now, but Clay and I wouldn't be going to bed for a while. I sat on the floor, my back to the wall, phone in hand. Clay paced. Or he did until I snapped at him that he was making me dizzy, and he snapped back with, "Well, at least I'm not sitting on the goddamn floor. What the hell are you doing? Giving yourself a time out?"

I ignored him and checked the phone.

"It rings when someone calls," he said. "Miracle of technology."

I got to my feet and stalked to the adjoining door. Clay cut me off before I got there.

"Where're you going?"

"To tell Nick to switch rooms with you. I get that you're exhausted, but I don't need you snapping at me."

"Pretty sure you started it."

"By asking you not to pace? Obviously I'm a little stressed and you're—" I sucked in breath. "I don't want to fight."

"We're not fighting."

I gave him a look. "I don't want to argue about whether we're fighting either. Once Jeremy calls, I'm going to ask you to switch rooms. You're angry with me. You have every right to be, and we'll hash it out later. Just not tonight. Please not tonight."

He stepped closer but I backed up and walked to the window, only to feel his hand on the back of my shirt.

"Right, right," I said. "Sorry. No windows."

He took my shoulder and turned me to face him. "I'm not angry. If I snapped about you sitting on the floor, it's because I know you're punishing yourself for this. Because Malcolm's back. Punishing yourself because we didn't stop him before he *came* back."

"Because *I* didn't stop him," I said. "You wanted to go after him. I refused. You were right, and you have every reason to blame me—"

"I have *no* reason to blame you, Elena, which is why I'm not. You made a decision as Alpha—"

"Which doesn't mean it's right," I said as I backed away. "Ascending to Alpha doesn't divinely imbue me with the ability to make smart choices. That's what I hate. Really, really hate. Worrying that even if you think I'm making the completely wrong decision, you'll support it, because you have to. The person I need to call bullshit on me the most—the one I've already relied on to do that most—is the one least likely to do it. I know it's your instinct to follow an Alpha, but I need things the way they were."

"Which is?"

"Which is you telling me when I have my head up my ass."

"Um, pretty sure I still do that. In fact, I did it last week when you decided to take Nick to England instead of me."

"That's different."

"Yeah, because there wasn't a *right* choice there. Just choices. Same as this, Elena. You didn't make the wrong choice. You made a choice. Did I really think I should be with you in England? Or did I just *want* to be? I don't know. As for Malcolm, sure, now we're kicking ourselves, but you had a good reason to not chase him. Because he came damned close to killing both Nick and Vanessa, and the only reason he failed is because he underestimated them both. If we chased him to Bulgaria, the chances we'd have lost a Pack member? Too damned high. If he was across the ocean, with a transmitter implanted, there was no reason to take that risk. Jeremy backed your decision. After I cooled down? I agreed, and I said so, and that wasn't because you're Alpha. I won't ever say it because you're Alpha. If I haven't made that clear by now…"

I exhaled and leaned against the wall. "You have. I'm just tired and I'm whining. I'm sorry."

"It's not whining, it's fretting. Which you do very well."

"I know. I have to get over it."

He moved to me, hands going to my hips. "The day you get over it, darling, is the day you won't be a damned fine Alpha. It's part of the package."

He leaned in to kiss me, but my phone rang. We both jumped. It was Jeremy's ringtone. I scrambled to answer.

It was a short conversation. Jeremy was as exhausted as the rest of us. The call was simply to say, "We're here and everything's fine." I wished him a good night, hung up and leaned back against the wall, exhaling, phone clutched in my hand. Clay pried it from my fingers and set it aside. His arms went around me, and I opened my eyes to see his face over mine.

"They're okay," I said.

"I know."

His mouth came to mine, and there was one brief moment where it was just a kiss, lips pressing together, a silent transition from the hell of the day to one moment of perfect peace. Then that passed with a crash, like a window smashing, hurtling through, grabbing each other hard, struggling for a hold.

I hit the bed. I didn't stay there, just hit it on the way down, catching the edge before continuing on to the carpet.

I didn't stay there, either. Not that I had any idea where I went—against the chair, against the wall, maybe even back on the bed momentarily. Deep, devouring kisses. Hands on clothes. Hands under clothes. Hands ripping clothes. No foreplay, no time or desire for it. Just need and grappling bodies and an endless kiss and finally *oh God, yes*, release, all the hell of that day dissipating in a few moments that reminded me I wasn't alone, would never be alone, never had to feel alone. No matter how bad things got, I had him. Always.

After, we lay on the floor, panting as we caught our breath. I surveyed the damage, mentally tallying the price tag. Yes, I can estimate damage costs in hotel rooms. Normally, if we're in one, we're on an investigation, which means tension and adrenaline is running high and, well, let's just say that's a good excuse to cut loose more than we can at home. It's never extensive damage—maybe a broken lamp or busted bedpost. The problem isn't so much the cost as having to explain to the desk clerk that we owe them for a lamp or bedpost. Clay handles that. He isn't bothered in the least. As he says, they shouldn't put so many damned lamps in hotel rooms anyway. Privately, I agree. They're very inconvenient.

"Bed?" he said.

"Mmm, please. The carpet..."

"Stinks."

"I was going to say 'smells a little off.' But yes, it reeks."

He scooped me up and tossed me into bed. Before he crawled in, he caught me surveying the room, and walked to the minibar. He grabbed all the snacks and two Cokes. He dumped the snacks on the bed, then set the cans on the nightstand.

"Mind reader," I said.

"No, just experienced. The first look around the room says, 'Shit, how much are we gonna owe?' The second one says, 'Damn, I'm hungry.' But only if the damage estimate is low enough that you can justify raiding the minibar."

I unwrapped a chocolate bar and devoured it in five seconds flat. A second followed. Clay finished off one as he crawled in, saying, "Better?"

"All around better," I said, falling back onto the pillow. "Thank you."

He pushed hair off my shoulder and kissed it. "Actually, that was my line. Thank you. For earlier."

"Mmm, pretty sure that was mutual."

A chuckle. "I'm talking about when you first arrived at the cabin. Thank you for not making me feel like I'd lost her."

"You didn't."

"It felt like I did, and I don't know what was worse, Kate being missing or me having to face you and say she disappeared on my watch."

I entwined my legs around his, getting closer as I buried my face against the side of his.

"I have nightmares about that," I whispered. "Something happening. Telling you."

"So do I. But if anything ever did? I'd never blame you. You're an amazing mother, Elena. You would do anything for them, and I don't ever doubt that."

"Ditto," I said.

He laughed softly and pulled me onto him. ⌒

Seventeen

*I*T WAS PROBABLY a damned good thing that Malcolm didn't see fit to attack us in the hotel that morning, or I suspect Clay and I would have provided very easy targets. After more sex, we'd zonked out, dead to the world. I managed to rouse once to check my phone. Jeremy had promised that whoever was on watch duty would send me hourly texts. I had four "All clear" messages. As soon as I read them, I collapsed back into bed.

I woke again when someone thudded down between us, hard enough to make me bounce. I opened one eye and peered over to see Nick stretched out in the middle of the bed.

"Good morning," he said.

I grunted and closed my eye. Clay didn't even stir.

"Rise and shine," Nick said, thumping the mattress with one hand.

"Go away."

"Time to get up."

I reopened my eye and glowered at him. "Did I give an order?"

"Didn't hear it. You're kind of mumbling. You seem a little tired."

My response was half grumble, half growl. He ignored the growl part.

"With all the noise in here last night, Morgan thought we should check, in case you were under attack. I said no, it was just sex. I don't think he believed me. It was a lot of noise."

"Invest in earplugs."

"Or you could just be, you know, quieter. More befitting your role as parents."

"That's why it's loud," Clay muttered, his eyes still shut. "Because we're parents, and we're not at home."

"You're also an old married couple. It should be quieter by now. More dignified."

I lifted my middle finger and shut my eyes.

"You broke a lamp," Nick said. "Again."

"Hmmph."

"How do you break a lamp during sex?"

"How do you not?" Clay mumbled.

The bedsprings squeaked as Nick sat up.

"You leaving?" Clay said. "Good."

"Nope, sorry. If I leave, you'll just decide you have enough energy for wake-up sex. So I'm staying."

"Might not stop us from having it," Clay said.

"That's why I'm *between* you two. I'm just getting up because, judging from the smell wafting through that connecting door, Morgan has returned with breakfast."

I inhaled and lifted my head.

Nick chuckled. "That got a reaction."

"Bring it in," I said. "Drop it off. Go."

"Is that an order?"

"Yes."

"Too bad. You're still mumbling. Morgan?"

"Yep."

"Come on in. Elena's going to get dressed and give us our orders while we eat."

STEP ONE: EAT breakfast.

Step two: issue orders.

Doing the two simultaneously wasn't an option. While perfectly capable of holding dinner conversations—often hours long—it's a different story when we'd spent yesterday wolfing down whatever was available. Morgan had gone to the Denny's in the hotel and ordered enough food for ten people. We devoured half of it before the planning started.

After breakfast, Nick and I had phone calls to make. Meanwhile Clay, Karl and Morgan would patrol the hotel and surrounding lot. They took off as soon as the last bite was finished.

I started with a call to Marko Todorov, leader of the Bulgarian Pack. Well, technically the Bulgarian Pack, though it also covered Macedonia and Albania.

The fact that Todorov wouldn't let me chase a killer through his territory should suggest he was a grade-A asshole who'd get along just great with Hollis John Parker. He wasn't. In fact, under any other circumstances, Todorov and I might have worked together just fine. The problem was he didn't trust Americans. I tried playing the "I'm Canadian" card. It didn't work. It rarely does.

To Todorov, Americans are imperialist bullies always looking for a takeover angle. He knows I have no interest in his territory—the American Pack has plenty of land. What we lack, though, is the wolves to properly protect it, so he's worried we might try to steal some of his.

It wasn't just mistrust of Americans that made Todorov refuse us access to his territory. He knew who Malcolm was. He knew who Clayton was. He didn't want the two of them going mano-a-mano on his land. He feared the fallout would include dead Bulgarian werewolves or an exposed Bulgarian Pack. I pointed out that Clay had been dealing with mutts for thirty years and had never been responsible for an exposure threat. I also offered to send Karl and Antonio instead. Todorov didn't trust that I wouldn't sneak over with Clay. Which proved he was a smart man.

Being smart, he also hadn't wanted to completely piss us off. So he'd given me his word that he would keep an eye on Malcolm's movements. If Malcolm left the country, I'd be the first to know.

Now I called and told him we had reason to believe Malcolm had left the country. Todorov said that wasn't possible—his wolves checked Malcolm's latest hideaway twice weekly, and he'd been there less than twelve hours ago. Todorov asked about the transmitter signal.

"It's still working," I said. "But I'm sure he's—"

"If the signal is still working, then he is still here."

"I smelled him in Vermont just last night."

"You are mistaken."

"Three of us smelled him, independently."

"Then Malcolm has another son who smells more like him. Not surprising, given how popular he seems to be with the ladies here." Todorov sighed. "One can never underestimate the appeal of, what do you call it? The bad boy?"

"Yes, Malcolm has no trouble with women, sadly, but this scent—"

"He is still here, Elena."

"Can you get me a photograph?"

A pause. "Are you accusing me of lying?"

"It's a favor, not an accusation. Do this for me and I'll owe you one. If there's a chance we're mistaken, though, I need to know—"

"You are mistaken."

"Okay, so a photo…"

"We are not servants of the American Pack."

"You are a fellow Pack, being asked for a favor, which we will repay—"

"I am going to hang up the phone now."

"Malcolm has werewolves with him. I think he brought them. And, no, I'm not saying they're your wolves, just that—"

"Do you know how many werewolves are on my territory who are *not* part of my Pack? Two. And only because we have no use for them, meaning Malcolm Danvers would not either. He did not take wolves from my territory."

"Because he's still there?"

A brief pause, where I'm sure if the line was better, I'd have heard Todorov curse. He came back with, "That is correct," but it was too late. He'd lost Malcolm, and he hadn't notified me, and now he was covering his ass.

"Thank you for your help, Marko," I said. "I'll remember it."

I hung up. ⌒

Eighteen

WHILE I'D BEEN talking to Todorov, Nick had been on the phone with Vanessa. He'd met her when he'd hired—on my order—a network of supernatural mercenaries to find Malcolm for us. I'd worked with the head of that organization in the past, so I had no qualms about subcontracting this particular task to them.

Vanessa's team had found Malcolm, and she'd gone after him with Nick. They've been together ever since.

Vanessa lives in Boston, which is only a few hours from the Sorrentinos, so Nick's probably there every other weekend. She's at his place less often, more aware that a werewolf's house is also his territory, and while the guys might say they're fine with having her there, until they're completely comfortable with her, it'll still feel like an intrusion. The comfort level is growing, though, as we begin to accept this might be the real thing for Nick. It helps that even Clay likes and respects her, and for werewolves, the latter is often more important than the first.

Once I got off the phone with Todorov, Nick stopped his conversation with Vanessa and said, "I'm going to put you on speaker with Elena."

We exchanged greetings. They were warm, if not particularly long or effusive, because we both wanted to get down to the important matter at hand. I think that's one reason I get along so well with Vanessa—we operate in much the same way. The brief exchange of greetings focused on our kids, Vanessa asking about the twins and me about her college-aged niece, who has lived with her since Vanessa's sister's death. That's one thing that helped cement her relationship with Nick—both had older "foster" kids and were devoted to them.

Once we'd exchanged familial check-ins, she asked, "How are things?"

"Okay. We're dealing."

"Anything I can do to help, just ask," she said and that was the extent of the discussion on last night's events. No expression of sympathy or concern because neither solved the problem and that's where our focuses were, always. "I told Nick I can be there in a few hours."

"I told her no," Nick said.

"I believe that's Elena's call," Vanessa said. "As Alpha."

"She's Alpha of me. Not you."

"Ah, so *you're* Alpha of me?"

Nick wisely didn't answer that. Vanessa chuckled and said, "Yes, I don't have an Alpha, but Elena is team leader here, and since I'm used to playing that role myself, I don't challenge the authority of the chick in charge. Nor should anyone else."

"I'm not—" He cut himself short and then shook his head in my direction, asking me to refuse her offer. For very good reason.

"I'm not eager to bring you in," I said. "You outwitted Malcolm. He's also probably figured out you were the one who planted that transmitter in him. You're on his shit list. You and Nick."

"All the better to put us together. I've watched Nick's back many times. I know how he operates, and he knows how I operate. We make a good team."

"You make a great team but—"

"Yes, I'm shit in a brawl. I'm an excellent shot, though, and I'm not ashamed of bringing a gun to a werewolf fight. You could probably use that."

"True but—"

"I've met Malcolm. I've fought him. Karl, Morgan, Reese... they can't say that. Even Antonio and Jeremy, as well as they knew him thirty years ago, they haven't had to deal with him now, and Nick says he's a whole lot worse."

"He is, which is why I'd rather not bring you in. Do you remember that fight?"

Silence. There was more to my words than Nick knew. A secret she hadn't told him about her fight with Malcolm. She was possibly regretting she'd told me, but I hoped not. She'd had to tell someone.

Nick knew only that Malcolm tried to kill her, which was a given. About a year ago, after one too many drinks, just the two of us, she'd confessed that Malcolm had given her a choice. He could kill her or break her spine, so she'd live, paralyzed from the neck down.

"I've dealt with killers before," she'd said, staring across the bar. *"If anyone else said that, I'd ignore it as an idle threat. But he meant it, and he had me in a position where I actually thought I'd have to make that choice. I have nightmares about that day. About him. About choosing. I always say, 'Kill me,' and that's what scares me most. The choice should be to live. No matter what, just live. But I...I don't think I could like that. I'd go mad."*

When I brought it up, she went quiet, her breathing picking up before she brought it under control.

"I remember," she said.

Nick glanced over, brow furrowing. I pretended not to notice.

"Then you'll understand why I'd rather not bring you in."

"Yes, and you'll understand why I need to. If I can have the chance to face him again? Just face him and get past that..."

Of every reason she could have given, that was the one I couldn't ignore. The rest was true, too, which didn't help. She was an ace mercenary, a born leader, a crack shot, and there was no one that I'd rather put at Nick's side. If I'm being honest, I'd rather have her there than Clay or myself. We're a little too protective of him. Vanessa only knew Nick as she saw him now, perfectly capable of holding his own and watching her back.

If we could use her, could I deny her the chance to face her demons? I knew what that was like, the gnawing fear that you have a weakness, one you could overcome if you had the chance.

I glanced at Nick. He rubbed his face, didn't look happy, but after a few moments, he nodded.

"Let us see what we can do this afternoon," I said. "If it looks like it'll go into the night, we'll bring you in. I'll let you know by dinner hour. Does that work?"

"It does. I'll drive into New York for the day and be ready. Thank you."

More business talk after that. The transmitter belonged to her organization so she'd get their technicians working on it, seeing if they could get any answers. More importantly, she'd already notified Rhys—her boss—that Malcolm was stateside. They'd drop whatever nonessential work they were doing to help us find him—hacking into the airlines to figure out which of his aliases he was using and tracking any other uses of it in the last twenty-four hours.

Rhys didn't drop everything to help us because he was a nice guy. He's a mercenary. Completely fair to deal with but not inclined to charity. He'd screwed up with Malcolm, though. The arrangement had been that Nick would be notified as soon as they found Malcolm. No one would go near him, even to make a definitive ID. Rhys had ignored that part. Clearly we'd been overreacting. His people would get close enough to get a picture, so there would be no chance Rhys was sending us on a wild goose chase. Malcolm had killed the trained operative who tried to get that photo. Stalked her, lured her, cut her throat and left her to bleed out slowly in an empty building.

Rhys's mistake had cost Vanessa one of her team members. Helping us on this was his way of making amends. I could say it wasn't his fault—he'd made a miscalculation that dozens of others had made in dealing with Malcolm. But letting him off the hook wouldn't help me, so I let him dangle.

*

AFTER THE CONVERSATION with Vanessa, we joined the others on patrol. Two hours later, Clay fell in step beside me and made a show of flashing his watch.

"I know, I know," I muttered. I'd said if we didn't have anything by noon, we'd move to step two. I really didn't want to move to step two.

"You think I want to use our kids as bait?" he said.

When I gave him a look, he nodded, "Yeah, okay. Goes without saying. My point is that Malcolm's not here, darling. He might be nearby watching us. But if so, he's not coming out of his hole until we give up and lead him to Jeremy and the kids."

"Maybe if we use Nick—"

"If that didn't work an hour ago, it's not working now. We've let Nick wander off. We've let you wander off. Malcolm's not biting."

He was right. Time to move to the next stage. ⌒

Nineteen

E SPLIT UP so if anyone was watching, it didn't look as if we were leading a convoy to a trap. Did I *hope* no one was watching? That Malcolm had retreated? No. As tempting as that was, I didn't want him going into hiding again. That route had led us to my daughter being out in the forest alone, stalked by the most dangerous werewolf in the world.

Manage the situation. That was all we could do. Which in this case meant acting as if we were damned certain we'd huffed and puffed enough to scare off the big bad wolf, and now we were picking up the kids and going home.

Jeremy met us in the parking lot. "Hope and Reese are with the twins," he said as we headed in.

"I wasn't asking."

"I'm still telling. Noah and Antonio are on patrol. I asked Hope to come in and help with the kids."

"Getting cabin fever, are they?" I said as we waited for the elevator.

When Jeremy didn't reply, I glanced up sharply at him. "Jer?"

He motioned to wait for the elevator. When it arrived, two young guys with sports bags stepped up behind us. Jeremy and I got on the elevator. Clay followed, said, "Full," and hit the button to close the door before the guys could even squawk in protest.

"Kate's having some trouble this morning," Jeremy said. "That's why I came down to meet you. She's fine; I would have called if she wasn't. But she's not up and running around, so I'm warning you now."

"Any symptoms?"

"Low-grade fever. Muscle aches. Nausea. If she was a normal child, I'd diagnose oncoming flu."

"Okay. When this is over, can you write me up a timeline? Symptoms to expect and how close that means we're getting?"

"I can..."

At his hesitation, I glanced over, and when I did, I caught Clay's expression, the worry darkening his eyes. He saw me looking and tried to cover it, but it was too late.

"How far along is she?" I asked carefully. "Restlessness and muscle twitches are the first signs, and she's only just started those..."

"The timetable appears to be accelerated," Jeremy said.

"What? How accelerated?"

When Jeremy didn't answer, Clay asked, "What's her temperature at?"

Jeremy pursed his lips.

"Jeremy," I said.

"A hundred and three."

"A hundred and— That's not low-grade—" I smacked the panel hard enough to make the elevator shudder. "Goddamn it, Jer. If she was feverish last night, you should have told—"

"She wasn't. It started about an hour ago."

"An hour ago? She's spiking a hundred and three temp, and she's up in a hotel room—"

"With Hope and Reese, who would call if anything happened. The fever will break soon. I could bring it down, but if I do, the cycle only repeats. It's a normal part of the process."

"How far along in the process?" I said, striding off the elevator as soon as the doors opened.

Jeremy steered me in the right direction and murmured the room number.

"That's not an answer."

"Because I don't have one."

"Is she vomiting?" Clay asked. "Or just feeling nauseated?"

"No vomiting. She's past the midway for the usual process, but this isn't the usual situation, so we can't expect that. She's handling it fine, Elena, and the reason we're having this conversation before you get to that door isn't because I'm preparing you for the worst. I'm preparing you not to panic when you see she has a fever. She's all right. Logan, however…?"

"He's worried," I said.

"Yes, and your worry only feeds his. As it always does."

"Right. Okay."

I reached the hotel room. The door was opening before Jeremy could get out his keycard. It was Reese. His face was drawn, mouth tight, but he forced a smile for me.

"Hey, hope you brought a deck of cards, because we have two very restless kids in here."

"How would cards help that?" Kate's querulous voice from the next room. "We need to get out."

"One's a little cranky, too," Reese whispered.

"I heard that!"

"You're supposed to!"

Logan came into the hall before I could continue into the room. If Reese looked drawn from worry, Logan looked carved from it, so brittle and tightly wound that when he gave me a quick embrace, I barely hugged him back, for fear of snapping something.

He high-fived Clay, which was his usual greeting these days. Normally, he did the "high, low, too slow" trick, and if we failed, he'd grin and tell us we were getting old, after which he'd have to dart out of the way, or we'd grab him and show him our reflexes were fine. A family routine, one of the few times our son acts his age, and sometimes I think he does it mostly for our benefit. Today, he didn't try to pull away his hand, which meant, "I'm trying to show you guys I'm okay, but I'm not really."

"Reese is right," he said as he led us into the main room. "She's cranky. I tried to swipe sedative from Jeremy's medical bag, but apparently, being a brat is"—he air-quoted—"not a medically-sound reason for tranq'ing her. He has a point. If we start that, we'll never stop. She'll spend her life sleeping."

"Ha-ha," Kate grumbled.

She sat cross-legged on the bed with Hope. They were playing a game on an iPad. When I walked in, Kate set it aside. Her face was red, her eyes fever-bright. When I put my hand to her forehead, I expected her to snap that yes, her fever hadn't miraculously vanished in the last five minutes, but she leaned against my hand, as if the cool touch was welcome.

"I think it's going down," she said. "Jeremy? Can you please check?"

I could interpret the polite request as meaning her temper *was* dropping, but no matter how cranky she got, she never snapped at Jeremy. He checked it and said yes, it was down a degree and a half.

"I really need to go for a walk," she said. "Jeremy said I could ask when you got here. Can we? Please?"

I looked at Clay.

"Dad can come to, if he has to," Kate said.

"Thanks," Clay drawled. "I guess we can, if we stick close to the hotel."

It might draw Malcolm out. We both knew that, even if we didn't dare say it, felt guilty for thinking it. But it had to be done, in whatever way worked. Deal with him now or we'd never stop dealing with him.

"Hope?" I said. "Can you call Karl? Tell him to stick with Morgan and send Nick to Antonio. Noah can join us on our walk."

Kate tapped my hand and shook her head. "I'd like to talk to you and Dad alone."

"All right. Reese? Can you go out and escort Noah back? Have him get some food and a rest. You and Hope do the same. You'll be going out next."

We got to the door, and Kate looked around, frowning as if she'd forgotten something. "Lo?" she called.

He peeked around the corner.

"Well, come on," she said.

"I didn't hear my invitation."

A near-growl, as if such an expectation was ludicrous beyond words. He grabbed his shoes.

OUR "WALK" CONSISTED of circling the building, while staying far from parked cars. Kate didn't argue. She talked to me about the Change. She'd spoken to Noah and gotten his experience, but her questions weren't so much about data as experience, and less on the process itself but what life would be like afterward. Would she feel different? Would she "change" in any way except the obvious?

For years, I told myself that the harsher aspects of my nature came from what Clay did to me. That was easier than admitting his bite had only lit a match to that tamped-down rage from my childhood. Instead of turning that anger inward and burning with it, as I used to, I vented it, sometimes snapping with ill temper and snarling in arguments, sometimes enjoying hunting a rogue mutt a little too much. When that rage was finally extinguished, I'd had to face the fact that this was me—I could be hard and violent and argumentative, and that was my nature, and not anything Clay had done.

Whatever Kate was, at her core, would not change. What did change were the tools she would have to act on her emotions. Shove her brother in anger, and she could break ribs. The wolf inside also subtly changed behavior. She'd develop wolf instincts. The instinct to chase anything that flees. The instinct to protect loved ones. The instinct to defend territory. All can have very serious consequences if they aren't controlled.

Kate knew all this from growing up in a family of were-wolves, and I was now happier than ever that we'd come "out" with the twins. She understood the dangers and the limitations we dealt with, and she wasn't asking about them as much as she was working through it all. Talking to Mom about it. Getting a handle on it.

Logan listened in silence. I wanted to speak to him privately about what he was going through. Not just concern over his sister, but the possibility that maybe, deep down, he was a little envious. Last night I'd briefly asked if he was experiencing anything. He wasn't. I didn't want to dwell on that, but I knew he might be experiencing something: emotions he'd rather not experience. He'd want to rise above this. Fret about his sister. Support her through it. Never say—never *feel*—anything that could approach, "Why not me?" I'd talk to him when I could.

We were making our fourth circuit when Hope came jogging around the side of the building. Karl followed at a brisk walk.

"Hey, sorry we're late," she called as she hurried over.

I had no idea what she was talking about, but given how loud her normally soft voice had gotten, someone was listening. I tried not to stiffen.

"We'll take the kids up to Jeremy," she said. "You guys get going. See if that lead pans out."

She drew close enough to lower her voice, "I caught a few stray chaotic thoughts. Someone's watching. Getting antsy and wondering why they can't strike and be done with it."

She laid a hand on Kate's shoulder. "So, are you up for another round of Battleship? Or are you afraid of losing again?"

Kate snorted. "I lost once. Out of five games."

"Mmm, pretty sure it was twice." Hope gave me a hug and murmured. "No idea where this guy is, but close enough to see you and the kids walking around." She pushed keys into my hand and whispered, "Reese's."

"Thanks."

Clay and I hugged Kate, patted Logan on the back and watched as Karl and Hope took them inside. Then we headed for Reese's pickup. ⌁

Twenty

EN MINUTES LATER, Clay and I were circling back toward the hotel on foot, having left Reese's truck half a mile away.

Hope had texted everything she'd "heard" in her vision. It gave me some idea where to find Malcolm's scout. I'd warned the others away from that area, so they wouldn't spook him. Essentially, he seemed to be holed up in a building nearby. His mental complaints put him in a dusty room, suggesting an unused building. There were no helpful abandoned ones around the hotel, but there was a rundown office building that looked as if it might have a vacancy or two. Better yet, sight-lines from the upper-floor windows would let him keep an eye on comings and goings at the hotel.

Being Sunday, the office building was empty—or close to it. I smelled the guy as soon as we entered through the back door.

The others would have patrolled past this building, but probably hadn't sniffed too hard. There were a few people around, which suggested it wasn't the best spot for Malcolm's minions. It also meant said minions couldn't walk around the building wearing carbon-lined jumpsuits. Not outside hunting season anyway.

"I know this scent," I said as I bent inside the back door.

Clay crouched while I peered down the dimly-lit hall. "Huh," he said.

"Translation?"

He straightened. "Same here, but I'm not placing it. I don't think I've met the guy. I've picked up the scent in the past. It's from…" He went still, thinking, then shook his head. "It's not coming, darling. I'll keep trying."

I followed the trail down the back hall. Which does not mean I crawled, nose to the ground, as charming a picture as that might make. I walked to the junction with the main corridor, then hunkered down to figure out which way he'd turned. Left. I made a few spot checks as we walked, with Clay watching to make sure no one walked in and saw me sniffing the floor. Which, might I point out, smelled like it hadn't been cleaned in years. But my nose is attuned to the bouquet of werewolf, so I found that thread.

The trail led to the stairwell, then up to the top floor, as we expected. Down the hall, testing each door. Office 504 was our winner.

"No balconies, right, darling?" Clay whispered against my ear.

I nodded.

"Large windows?"

I paused, then whispered back, "You might want to go down. To be sure."

He considered that. Last night, I'd accused him of agreeing with whatever I said because I was Alpha. Obviously bullshit, but when you're caught up in a state of mind, you ignore evidence that contradicts your theory. Clay was beta and my bodyguard. I could tell him to go downstairs and watch the front of the building—in case this guy leaped out the window—but he was still going to weigh the pros and cons—how much danger did I face alone versus how much flight risk did this guy pose—before he agreed. Yes, he agreed with my decision 99.9 percent of the time, but he did always consider it, proving he wasn't just blindly obeying. And to suggest he did? Insulting, really.

It only took about ten seconds for him to nod. While he wasn't keen on leaving me to fight an unknown enemy, it was one werewolf—and definitely not Malcolm. I could handle it. And that risk of flight-through-a-convenient-window? High. Hell, the first time I met Reese he'd jumped off a roof. Give a guy super-strength and reflexes, and sometimes he's not going to use it to fight—he's going to use it to make a death-defying plunge to safety.

Clay left. I stood at the door to 504. The room on the other side was so silent that I began to wonder if the guy wasn't there. That's the problem with scent. For all I knew, I'd been following an exit trail.

Then footsteps sounded inside. Footsteps heading straight for the door. It hadn't been enough time for Clay to get into position so I backed up and pressed against the wall, so anyone coming out of the room wouldn't see me right away.

The door opened. A man stepped out. He saw me and froze, his nostrils flaring, double-checking what his eyes told him. His lips formed a, "Fuck." Then he looked behind me. They *always* look behind me.

"Where is he?" the werewolf asked. As soon as I heard his accent I also recognized his scent. He was a British Pack wolf. I'd seen him on my last visit with Clay, but briefly and had never been introduced.

"Where—?" he began again.

"Close," I said. "Clay's always close. If you'd rather just deal with me, let's step back into that room and you can tell me why your Alpha sent you to spy on my Pack."

The chances that Parker had just happened to send a spy at the same time Malcolm appeared with unknown were-wolves? Zilch. But I was giving this guy a reason to think he could lie his way out of this. He started to nod when there was a click behind me, like a door opening down the hall.

The door never opened—it was just a fan or something coming to life—but the Brit didn't even pause long enough to get a look. He heard that click, and he raced back into the office. I grabbed the door and tore in after him. By the time I was through, he was already in the next room, holding an office chair, poised at the window, ready to slam it through.

"That's where he is," I said quickly.

"What?"

"You're looking for Clay? He's down there. If you really want to jump on top of him—"

The guy whammed the chair into the window. It shattered, the chair and glass falling through. The Brit poked his head out.

"Don't see him," he said. "But nice try."

He jumped through. I raced around the desk and reached the window to see him running. With no one chasing.

"Shit!"

I leaped through the broken window.

*

I'D WARNED THE British wolf about jumping through and landing on Clay. Which is what I nearly did. Clay emerged from the other side of the building just as I leaped. Luckily, he saw the chair and the glass and looked up before we collided.

I hit the ground hard but landed right, which is always a concern. We aren't cats. There's a damn good chance we won't land on our feet. I did. Unfortunately, so had the British werewolf, and he was running unimpeded for the parking lot.

Clay was hot on the guy's trail. Or warm. He was at least two hundred feet behind, and whatever Clay's skills might be, he won't ever win a sprint. I passed him in a few strides, but with the Brit's head start, all he had to do was run straight to the parking lot, jump into his car and tear off.

I took a flying leap at the car as he gunned it. My fingers grazed the trunk—and I fell flat on my face as it roared off. Like I said, we're wolves, not cats.

Clay helped me up. I brushed myself off and squinted at the disappearing car.

"Make, model and plate?" I said.

"Yep." Meaning he got it. Not that I suspected it would help much, but it was something.

I texted Jeremy as we headed back to the hotel. ⌐⌐

Twenty-one

EN MINUTES LATER, I was in the adjoining suite, so the kids couldn't overhear, which was useless, given that they have super-powered hearing and I was snarling into a phone behind a thin wall. My only consolation was that they couldn't possibly have lived with us for nearly nine years and never heard these particular words.

The first words that left Parker's mouth, after I blasted him? "I don't know what you're talking about." Also the second set of words. The third set. And the fourth.

I took a deep breath. "Let's start back at the simplest, most inarguable issue. One of your wolves is on my territory."

"No, he isn't."

"No, he isn't here? Or no, it's not my territory? If either of those statements dares leave your mouth—"

"None of my wolves are currently in America."

"So you're telling me this guy's no longer a Pack member?"

"I'm telling you exactly what I'm telling you, Elena. That you are mistaken."

"That the guy I saw a few minutes ago isn't the same one I saw in England three months ago?"

"That is correct."

"All right." I relaxed my stranglehold on the phone before it snapped in two. "So, three months ago, Clay and I met with you. A guy walked in. About thirty. Light hair. Short beard. He whispered something to you. Clay was closer and says he was updating you on a mutt issue in Manchester. Today, both Clay and I found his trail here. We then both saw him. I spoke to him. This guy, however, is not the one we saw in London with you."

"That is correct."

"Last night, a werewolf broke into our cabin and terrorized our son. I caught a whiff of scent I also recognized as it belongs to *another* member of your Pack."

"Yet you didn't contact me. In fact, as I hear, you made the same accusations to Marko Todorov earlier today. You said his wolves had joined up with Malcolm."

"Because while I recognized the scent at the cabin, I couldn't place it until I met the wolf today and it clicked."

Silence for five seconds. Then, "May I suggest, Elena, that you are reacting to this as the mother of endangered children, not as—"

"Nope, you may not. And I'd strongly suggest you don't try."

"But I must, because I'm quite surprised Jeremy allowed you to make this call. I presume he knows about it?"

"I'm right here," Jeremy said. He was beside me, listening, while Clay was in the next room with the kids.

"It's good to hear from you, Jeremy. You've been sorely missed."

I tried not to grind my teeth.

The lack of a polite response—or any response—from Jeremy was about as clear a "fuck you" as my former Alpha could give, but Parker didn't know him well enough to realize that, and when Jeremy didn't answer, Parker only continued.

"I understand that you're trying to provide Elena with the authority she needs to run your—I mean, her—Pack. That is commendable. But I'm sure you realize she's stepped into a political quagmire here, accusing two Alphas of collaborating with a known sociopath—" A pause. "My apologies if that designation is offensive."

"No designation you give my father is offensive. Please, continue." Any wolf in the American Pack would hear the tone of those last two words and shut his mouth fast. Parker did not.

"She has accused two Alphas of collaborating with Malcolm based on no proof, fueled merely by the hysteria—"

I had to swallow a growl.

"—the hysteria of seeing her children endangered. Naturally, as a mother, she is distraught and not thinking clearly. But as an Alpha, she will not be allowed to claim motherhood as an excuse for making groundless accusations. Granted, being the first female Alpha, there is no precedent for you—or her—to rely on, but let me assure you, she will not be relieved of responsibility for this accusation merely because of her gender."

"I would expect no less," I said. "In fact, if you were to relieve me of responsibility for any of my actions, based on my gender, *that* would be considered *extremely* offensive. If you are accusing me of making an inaccurate identification of your wolf because of hysterics, remember I'm not the only one making the ID. Are you accusing Clayton of hysteria too?"

Silence.

"I didn't think so. Nor would I suggest you want to accuse him of blindly seconding everything his mate says because she's the Alpha. We saw your wolf. I spoke to him. We have tracked the license plate of his rental car to a British citizen named Thomas Malloy."

"I have no wolves by that name."

"Presumably, he's not using his real one. While you might not be able to recall the aliases used by all your wolves, I bet you have those records."

"It's not my wolf."

"Are you sure? If I describe him again, in more detail, could you check that he's around?"

"Are you implying I don't know the whereabouts of my wolves? Careful, Elena. You are treading on increasingly unstable ground."

"How about a deal? Verify his whereabouts and give me your absolute assurance he's there, and you can have Karl Marsten to babysit your son for the entire school year."

His voice chilled. "I know where my wolves are. Asking me to check is an insult. Offering to bribe me to do it doubles that insult."

"Then I've insulted you. Doubly. I don't withdraw the insult—or the offer. In fact, I'll add to it. If I catch any of your wolves on my territory in the next forty-eight hours, your son is not welcome in the States. He will be treated as a trespassing member of a foreign Pack."

"Is that a threat?"

"Sounds like it. Does that triple the insult?"

Parker hung up.

I turned to Jeremy. "So, how badly did I mess up?"

"You haven't made an ally. However, considering your chances of that already seemed nonexistent, you're no further behind. You have delivered a message. If I thought it was an unreasonably dangerous one, I'd have stopped you."

"Only reasonably dangerous then?"

"Something like that."

I plunked onto the bed. "Either he's teamed up with Malcolm or his wolves have gone rogue. Care to lay bets on which it is?"

"No, but I would bet my bank account that it's one or the other. You and Clay saw exactly who you think you saw."

"Meaning now we need to catch one of them and prove it. Before Parker recalls them to England and I lose all credibility internationally."

"Something like that." ⌒

Twenty-two

I SENT ANTONIO AND Morgan to JFK. That's where our spy had rented his car, and I was betting Parker's wolves were hightailing it out of the U.S. I'd bought tickets to get the guys through security to wait for them.

That presumed Parker would recall his troops *and* that he'd actually sent them. If they were acting independently, his calls would go unanswered. However, if they'd gone rogue, then I very highly doubted their new boss would let them hightail it anywhere. They had a job to do.

I let the guys—and Hope—take it easy until nightfall. Insisted on it, actually. After that scare with the scout, Malcolm would wait for dark. Then he'd get bolder. I was sure of it, because that's what I'd do. I patrolled myself, switching among Clay, Karl and Hope as my second. Once it got dark, I sent everyone out and stayed with the kids.

The others had barely left when I came out of the bathroom and found Kate at the balcony window.

"Hey!" I said.

Logan jumped from the bed, where he'd been reading, and pulled Kate back.

"Sorry, Mom," he said. "I didn't see her."

"You shouldn't need to," I said, walking over. "Your sister is quite old enough to follow instructions. Did I tell you to stay away from the windows, Kate? In fact, if you know we're lying low in here, *should* I need to tell you?"

"I just wanted to…"

Her gaze swung back to the open curtains and the night beyond, and her eyes glittered like a drunk spotting a bottle. I yanked the drapes shut.

"I know," I said. "Tomorrow you'll be at home, and we'll walk in our forest all night if it makes you feel better. But tonight you need to control it."

She stepped back toward the drapes.

"Kate!" I said.

She turned to me, petulant. "I wasn't going to open them. I just…"

"Just what?"

A moment of silence. Then a sigh, her gaze dropping. "Okay, yeah. It's—it's hard."

I pulled her into a quick hug. "I know, baby. But it's only one night." I tugged her to the bed and sat her on the other side, facing away from the window. "Reese bought cards, so let's play something."

"Can we open the window?"

"That'll only make it worse."

She nodded. "I'm sorry, Mom. It's just…

"Hard?"

A faint smile. "Yeah."

Another hug, and we started playing. It didn't help. Kate was distracted and after the first round, she began rubbing her arms. She pulled off the hoodie she'd been wearing against the hotel air-conditioning, and as she did, her face flushed, and she started panting.

"Logan?" I said. "Can you—?"

He grabbed the bucket of half-melted ice and was in the bathroom before I could finish. I took hold of Kate's arm. The skin pulsed, muscles shifting beneath it. When I rubbed, I felt hair.

"Mom?"

Kate had her other arm lifted to eye level. We could see the hair now, golden fur poking through the skin, then retracting.

"That's normal," I said.

She started madly scratching.

"So's that."

"I know," she said, between pants, her face red with fever. "It just—it itches. Damn, it itches." Another mad scratching fit, then her gaze lifted to mine. "Sorry."

"A Change is the one time cursing is allowed. Possibly even encouraged."

Logan shot from the bathroom, a dripping, ice-cold towel in each hand. I stretched one over her arms and pressed the smaller one to her face.

"I could get more ice," Logan said. "But I don't think you want me going into the hall."

"No, I don't. Call—"

Logan scratched one arm through his hoodie. I reached for it, but he pulled back, making a face.

"It's an itch, Mom."

"Let me—"

"Mom. I'm not going to spend the next five years having you check me every time I scratch my arm."

"I know, but—" I exhaled. "Okay, call Jeremy. Tell him what's happening. I need him back here and—"

Kate let out a howl and the cloths fell. I grabbed her by the shoulder and pressed one cloth to her forehead. Her back contorted, muscles pressing against her T-shirt as she doubled over. I held her, rubbing her back and saying, "It's okay. It's okay," telling myself it was, that these were all normal stages, which would be true...if they'd been taking place over the last six months.

But they were still normal. Every one of them. Progressing in the proper order, and she was handling them like a pro. It was just bad timing. Really, really bad timing—

"Mom?" Logan held out my phone. "They're blocking the signal."

I took it, my first impulse being: *He's mistaken*. Which goes to show how scattered my mind was. He was right, of course. No phone signal. Full battery. I turned the phone off and on. No change.

"Shit?" he said. When I gave him a look, he lifted his brows innocently. "Just beating you to it."

Kate still lay in my arms, quiet now, shuddering and catching her breath as the convulsions passed. When I rubbed her back, she straightened and pushed blond curls out of her face with an impatient hand.

"We have to leave now, right?" she said.

I hesitated.

"They've killed our cell phones, Mom," Logan said, gently. "Next step: get the heck out, because killing the phones signals imminent attack. Right?"

Kate straightened and reached for her hoodie.

"Don't—" I began, about to tell her not to overheat by putting it back on, but she was tying it around her waist.

"I'm good, Mom," she said. "It's passed for now."

We should go while it had. I knew that, but I still looked at the hotel phone. While it was probably working, I'd need to call everyone out there in hopes of finding one who was out of signal-blocking range.

I got to my feet. "Have either of you heard anyone in the rooms on either side of ours?"

They shook their heads. The hotel was nearly empty, being Sunday night and past prime holiday season.

"Do we hide in the one to the left or right?" Logan asked, guessing my plan.

"Neither. They'll know the rooms aren't occupied, meaning that's where they'll set up base before they pounce. I heard people across the hall, but it's been quiet for a while." I checked my watch. "Too early for bed. They must be out for dinner. We'll use theirs while I start calling the others."

I was already in the entryway, whispering as I walked. I could have kept my thoughts to myself, but no teaching opportunity should be wasted. That's what the wolf in me says. The human says I'd rather be teaching my kids algebra, but agrees this will probably stand them in better stead. And I'm much better at this than algebra.

I popped open the door, sniffed, listened and then poked my head out. I thought I caught the scent of a werewolf, but very faint, as if he'd walked past the room a while ago.

I motioned to the kids to wait. I had Logan keep the door propped open while I darted across the hall. I pressed my ear to the other door. No one moved or spoke inside during the few seconds I dared wait before I snapped the lock. Luckily, the privacy latch wasn't fastened, suggesting I was correct and the occupants were out.

Holding open the other door, I motioned the kids over. I pulled them through and then—

"Mom?" Logan backed up so fast he plowed into Kate, who smacked into me, and we stumbled back like dominos. A door opened down the hall.

Footsteps sounded in the corridor. Heavy footfalls. Male. I caught a whiff of werewolf and closed the door quickly and quietly.

A stink hit me then, from inside the room. That's what had stopped Logan. I took a deep breath. Shit. No, not a curse—that's what I smelled. Feces and urine and blood. The stink of sudden and violent death. I flipped the privacy latch as quietly as I could.

"Wait here," I whispered.

Kate looked ready to argue, but Logan nodded and put his hand on her arm, as much to restrain her as to tell me he would.

I crept into the bedroom. There, on the bed, lay a couple not much out of their teens. Partially dressed. Beer bottles and chip bags and a pizza box littered the floor, along with a couple of condom wrappers. A young couple sneaking off to an out-of-the-way hotel for an evening together. A young couple who now lay facedown with their necks snapped. The young man had died quickly—he'd have been attacked first, targeted as the greater threat. The girl had fought. That's where the smell of blood came from. He'd grabbed her by the arm, shoved her face down on the pillow to stifle her cries, and broken her arm so hard bone jutted through. Then he'd snapped her neck.

"Mom!"

Logan's cry came just as I saw a blur of motion. A man leaping from the bathroom. Both kids were already in flight, charging their attacker. Which apparently wasn't the reaction he expected from two children, because he stumbled in surprise, making my tackle easy. I landed on top of him. The smell of werewolf filled my nose. It was the same one I'd smelled at the cabin.

I had him pinned on his stomach. He bucked and writhed. Normally, the end-game would be obvious. Trespassing werewolf threatening my kids? Now flat on his stomach? I should grab his hair and wrench, treating him to the same fate as those poor kids on the bed. Snap the man-killing bastard's neck.

I would have too, in a heartbeat, if my kids weren't right there, watching. Which meant I had to knock him out. That was a whole lot harder to do from this position. Especially when I sure as hell wasn't letting him get up when he was almost within arm's-length of my children.

We grappled as I tried to flip him around and drag him back into the bathroom. He knew what I was doing and punched, kicked and bit to avoid it. Meanwhile, my darling, endangered children discussed the unfolding action, as calmly as golf commentators.

"We should keep him alive to question him," Kate said.

"Mom's not going to kill him."

"Why not?"

"She doesn't have to. He's not a very good fighter."

The guy snarled and tried to hit a little harder at that.

"He lacks technique," Logan continued. "That's what Dad would say. On a scale, he's between Noah and Morgan. Closer to Noah."

"But he's gotta be twice Noah's age."

"I know."

"That's embarrassing."

"It is. Mom would finish him off a lot faster, except I think she's trying to knock him out. That's tough. She needs a hard surface to do it."

"But if she knocks him out, she can't question him."

"Given the time constraints, she doesn't have much choice. If he's staked out this room and they've shut down our cell phones, they plan to strike any minute now. The goal is to incapacitate him." The squeak of a shoe as I slammed the guy through the bathroom doorway. "You need help with that, Mom?"

I may have growled a somewhat impolite answer, the upshot being that I absolutely did not and they were to stay exactly where they were.

I got the guy over to the tub, wrapped my hands in his hair and bashed his head. The first time, he twisted sideways and got a bloody nose instead. I may also have dislodged a tooth or two. The second time, I managed it. Then I crouched there, panting. Knocking targets unconscious may seem the simple solution, but in truth, killing them is easier.

I rose and wiped blood from a cut over my eye.

"Good job, Mom," Logan said. "Eight out of ten."

I walked out of the bathroom. "Eight?"

"You lost one point at the beginning when you had him pinned." Logan backed up to let me into the entryway. "He managed to get an arm free and—"

He stopped. His lips formed an "O" and I followed his gaze... into the bedroom. I lunged to block his view of the dead couple.

"He killed...?" Logan began, his brow furrowed, question left dangling.

Kate tried to walk past, but we both stopped her.

"What?" she said. Then she looked at her brother. At his expression. Her nostrils flared. And she stopped in mid-step, her gaze swinging to me.

"The people who had this room…" she said.

I nodded.

"But why?"

"Because it's easier," Logan said, and a chill ran through me as his words echoed what I'd just thought a minute ago. *Why not just incapacitate them? Because killing them was easier.*

Kate's gaze moved to the bathroom doorway. She looked at the werewolf unconscious in the bathroom. "That makes him a man-killer. He has to die for that, doesn't he?"

I went still. "It's…more complicated than that."

"Is it because we're here?" Logan said.

"Can we discuss this later?"

"But if he's murdered—?"

"We will discuss this later," I said, enunciating each word. "I promise. Right now, I need to get you two out of here."

They looked at the door.

"No," I said. "Not that way. Kate, are you okay to go out the window? It's three floors."

She nodded. "I feel fine now."

"There's an office building a few hundred feet away. That's where we're headed. I should be able to call someone from there. If not, they can follow our trail and find us."

"The Pack?" Logan said. "Or Malcolm's guys?"

"Both, unfortunately. Now, wait here a second."

I headed into the bedroom and grabbed the discarded comforter from the floor.

"Mom," Kate said. "You don't need to cover—"

"I am," I said, and continued to the bed to shield the bodies from my children. ⌒

Twenty-three

WE WENT OUT the balcony doors and jumped off the side, as I did my best to keep us from being spotted by anyone behind the hotel. We made it across the field and to the office building. Partway there, I caught sight of a figure. It might have been one of my guys, but the wind was blowing in the wrong direction and he was too far to see his features. I shuttled the kids into the office building.

I chose my hiding place with care. Third floor, like our hotel, which had proved an easy leap, yet no one could climb up the sheer wall to reach us. I picked a suite at the rear, which got us as far from the hotel as possible and left open land for an escape route. It was a big office suite with multiple rooms, where I could put the kids in one *without* a window. I sat them down, retreated and stood facing the exit door as I made my phone calls.

Jeremy, Clay, Nick, Karl, Hope, Reese, Noah…I went down my list. Nine numbers. No answers. Whatever blocked my phone at the hotel still extended close to this range and my own service faded in and out, from a single bar to none and I had to keep repositioning myself to connect. I sent texts to Jeremy, Clay, Nick and Karl. I tried Antonio and Morgan, at the airport, but neither picked up. I phoned Jaime. No answer, and that wasn't a shock. She had a show tonight. Next I tossed a mental coin between Charlie and Madison. Technically, Charlie was the Pack candidate. He should be the one I called with a job. But while he seemed perfectly reliable, my fingers dialed Madison's number instead, which I suppose told me all I needed to know about whether I considered her a candidate, too.

Madison was doing homework. She'd started college last year, as she tried to figure out the direction her new life in America might take. I gave her the briefest description of the situation and told her to continue calling my nine numbers. Eventually, one of them had to step outside the blocked range.

I was finishing my call when a yowl from the kids' room had me hanging up with barely a goodbye. I jammed the phone into my pocket and raced into the room to find Kate on the floor in a fetal position, her spine and shoulder blades jutting against her shirt. Logan crouched beside her.

"It just started," he said. "It's coming fast."

I pulled off her shirt. Her contorting muscles didn't just ripple—they seemed to swim under her skin, moving fast and hard, rearranging themselves, preparing for the change of form. Fur pushed up a half-inch, then retracted. Kate let out a howl, loud enough to reverberate through the room.

"Mom, she can't—"

"I know." I took her shirt and held it against her mouth. "Bite down on this, baby. Go ahead and scream. Make as much noise as you need to. I'll deal with it."

Her eyes rolled. Sweat dripped from her face. Her eyes blazed with pain and fever and fear, but she nodded and clamped down on the shirt. Her whole body convulsed, rearing, spine bowing, vertebrae poking up, sweat pouring off her, and this was normal, for us it was normal, but to see it with a child, with *my* child…

I cursed Clay. Cursed him for what he'd done to me as I hadn't cursed him since those early days, when I'd been the one lying there, racked with fever and nightmare and agony. More than that, though, I cursed myself. Even as the thoughts passed through my brain, I banished them. Because what was I really saying? That I didn't want to be what I was? To have this life? To have made this choice—having children, knowing this could be the result? At the heart of it, what was I really saying? That I wished my children hadn't been born? Never.

This wasn't about what Clay had done or what I'd done. It wasn't about us. Kate was the one suffering. So the rest got shoved aside as I held her and rubbed her and told her it would be okay, that this would pass and it would be magical when it did, that she would become something beyond imagining, and once she did, she'd never wish for any other life. And I meant it. For perhaps the first time I really meant it.

"I'm going out," Logan whispered when Kate stopped groaning enough for me to hear him.

"No, you have to—"

"Just into the hall, Mom."

"I—"

"I'll be careful."

He stepped out without waiting for an answer. My phone buzzed. I grabbed it out as fast as I could. I saw the name and hesitated.

Vanessa? Why would she be—?

Shit, yes! Nick had called her at dinner and told her to head up. She was supposed to phone when she got close.

I hit the answer button.

"Hello?"

Silence.

"Hello?" I said, again, louder. I checked to be sure I hadn't hit mute in my haste. Or, worse, ignore. But no, I saw the timer counting. Then it stopped. The call ended.

I frantically hit redial. Nothing happened. No bars. I'd lost service. I got to my feet. Kate let out a muffled yowl. I stuffed the phone into my pocket again as I dropped beside her.

I hugged her and I rubbed her back and I told her it would be okay. There was nothing more to do. I told myself it was a false start, that it would stop and revert, and this was just an overdose of stress, and she'd be fine, just fine, months away from a transformation, and the truth was, I was full of crap. Her bones were crackling and her muscles pulsing and her entire body reconfiguring itself and all I could think was, "Holy shit, I have no idea what I'm doing."

My baby was turning into a wolf, and I didn't know how to help her. I'd never watched a full transformation. I'd experienced it only from her position, down on all fours, blinded by pain.

So work with that. Just work with that.

I helped her get into position, explaining as I went, hoping she heard me but even if she didn't, she let me put her on her hands and knees, tug off her shoes, rip off her jeans when they wouldn't come loose, her thighs already bunched into haunches.

"Lo," she said panting, words barely intelligible, her vocal cords shifting. "Logan."

"He's outside, baby. Just outside. He's fine."

"Lo, Lo, Lo…"

She wanted her brother. There was a split second where I wondered if having him see her like this wouldn't do more harm than good. If the situation was reversed, I don't think I'd have let her in. As tough as my little girl is, she's the sensitive one, too, the emotional one. Her brother had stopped her from seeing those bodies for good reason. Yet if it had been reversed, if Logan were the one Changing for the first time, he'd never have asked for her. However much it might have helped to have her by his side, he wouldn't want her traumatized—it would only have added to his own anxiety. But he'd want to be here for her, however upsetting it was to see his sister between forms and in agony.

"Logan?" I called.

"I'm fine," came the muffled answer.

"Kate wants you."

"Shhh. Someone's out there."

"Just—"

"I'm fine, Mom. Shhh." A pause, then. "Please."

Damn it. I looked from Kate to Logan and back. I wanted to give her what she needed right now, anything to ease the pain and console her, but Logan was being logical. *Someone's out there.* We had to be quiet, and he had to stay in position, listening.

Kate let out a garbled cry as her face started changing. Her eyes rolled, wild with terror. Any thoughts of her brother had evaporated. It was that moment in the process where the world could explode and I wouldn't notice, wouldn't care, absolutely consumed by one thought, "Just be over. Please, please be over."

Finally, it was. My daughter was gone, and in her place, I had a wolf. Not a pup, but a young wolf. She had fur nearly the same golden color as her father's, and bright blue eyes. A young wolf, perfect in every way, and I stared at her the way I'd stared the first time she'd been laid in my arms, marveling, awestruck.

I reached one tentative hand to touch her side, ready to pull back if she snapped or snarled. When I first began Changing—hell, for the first dozen years—I couldn't stand to be touched or petted by someone in human form. But I suppose that only shows my own discomfort with the dual form. When I touched Kate's heaving side, her fur unbelievably soft, she raised her head and whined and I started pulling back, but she stretched over, eyes closing with the effort, and nudged my hand. Wanting more of my touch. More of my comfort. I stroked and petted her and told her how perfect she was, how beautiful and how powerful, and she lay there, eyes closing as she panted, utterly exhausted.

Then her head shot up. Her gaze swung to the door. She whined, eyes open and anxious.

"Logan's out there," I said. "I can hear him." He must have been pacing, because I picked up soft thumps, like irregular footfalls. Logan wasn't a pacer, wasn't restless like his sister, but her situation would make him anxious.

She whined again, sharper now, and I smiled.

"I'll get him for you. You two can have a minute together while I stand watch."

As I headed for the door, I remembered what Logan had said. That he'd heard someone in the hall. That hadn't really penetrated. Well, yes, it had, but in my confusion, worrying about Kate, I'd been thinking that I already knew there were mutts in the building. The *hotel* building. We weren't in the hotel anymore.

I scrambled out of the office and spun to the hall door to see—

Logan was gone. ⌒

Twenty-four

LOGAN.

Where—

A moan sounded behind me, so soft it seemed like the wind through an open window. I turned and peered into the dark office.

Logan.

I raced down the hall and into the main office and saw—

An empty office.

Oh, shit. Oh, shit, shit, shit—

Another moan pierced the shouting in my head. Still soft, but with an edge. An edge of pain that I recognized as my son's as surely as if I heard his voice.

The sound came from behind a desk. As I ran toward it, scenarios flashed through my head. Logan, attacked while I'd been preoccupied with Kate. Logan, calling for help, me deafened to everything except Kate's stifled howls. Logan, *not* calling for help, stoically defending himself so I could stay with his sister when she needed me.

Of all the scenes I imagined, none included the one I found. Logan, on the other side of that desk, lying in the darkness, clothing neatly piled beside him as he lay on his side, convulsing and contorting with his own Change. Making no sound except those soft moans as sweat ran off him in rivulets, soaking the carpet.

I fell to my knees beside him and hugged him. He wriggled free, panting, "Kate? Is Kate—?"

"She's fine, baby. She did it. She Changed. She's resting."

"G-good." He shivered and ground his teeth.

"When—?"

"Earlier."

"Why—?"

"I've got it…under control."

"You've got it under control?" I hiccupped a laugh. "You're Changing into a wolf, baby. This isn't something you do by yourself."

"Dad did." He growled, deep in his throat, as if swallowing a wave of pain. When he spoke again, the words came rough, harsh, forced out. "Wasn't bad. Kate worse. No fever. Just felt…off. Itching. Muscles. She needed you. I was fine."

I remembered Kate jumping up, mid-transformation, calling for Logan. Not wanting him with her, but knowing he was going through the same thing and trying to tell me. That's what I'd heard in the next room. The start of his Change.

I'm fine, he'd said. That's what he'd meant. *I'm fine. Stay with Kate.*

I hugged him again. He let me, leaned against me even, shaking and shivering. I rubbed his back and I got him into position and I put something in his mouth and told him to stop being so damned brave about it. He gave a chuckling growl, accepted the cloth to bite on and let himself make a little more noise, the moans rising to stifled grunts and snarls.

Yes, it might have been less painful for him than for his sister. He hadn't had the preliminary fevers or the mood swings. But if it was better, that was relative, and it was by no means easy or painless. The sweat pouring from him and his rolling eyes told me that. I was calmer, too, though. I'd seen Kate through it, and she was fine, and he would be too. I talked to him and massaged his muscles and held him in position when he threatened to topple.

His transformation was no faster than Kate's, but it progressed just as perfectly. When he'd finished, he dropped onto his side and let me pet him and tell him everything was fine, he was just tired, rest now. Once his blue eyes closed, I hurried back to Kate. She was sound asleep.

I carried her into the other room with her brother. She roused enough to see him there, as I lowered her, and she lifted her head, gaze traveling over him. A soft snort of relief, seeing him Changed successfully, and when I laid her down, she rolled over to curl up against him. His eyes opened and he shifted, inching closer, nose buried in the fur at the ruff of her neck.

I eased back and exhaled, feeling as if I'd Changed myself, every muscle aching. The office went silent, and that's when I heard it. The squeak of a footstep in the hall beyond the suite.

"Follow the damn trail," a man said, his voice vaguely familiar.

"I'm trying," came the snarled reply.

Logan had said he'd heard someone. Apparently, he hadn't just said that to keep me with Kate and hide his own Change.

Now I listened as two British-accented voices argued over the trail. I hadn't been foolish enough to lead the kids straight in here. Our trail ran up to every door. I'd broken open a few and led the kids inside, further muddying our route.

The two men were trying doors now. Which would slow them down, but it wouldn't stop them. Eventually they'd find the right one and…

I looked at the twins. Sound asleep. Utterly exhausted. In absolutely no shape to leap out a window.

Footsteps approached the door of the office suite. They stopped. The handle turned. Logan let out a whimper, twitching in his sleep. I scrambled over and dropped beside him, my words more breath than sound.

He went quiet, still asleep. The handle twisted again.

"This one's locked," the man said. "But I think I heard something."

"Break it open then."

The lock snapped. I crept into the hall, tensed, ready to—

"Hold on," the second man called. "I've got something down here."

"But—"

"Who's in charge here?" I recognized the voice now. I'd spent two days in meetings with the man, though I'd rarely heard him speak. Shane Atherton. Parker's beta.

The first man left with a grumble. I considered. Then I hurried back toward the twins. They were hidden behind the desk and there was plenty of room for a knock-down brawl without ever getting near them. Good.

I returned to the door between the hallway and the main office and positioned myself behind it. Take out the first one through. Break his neck. No time to worry about my kids' sensibilities now. Their lives were more important.

In the Alpha's absence, the beta took his place, meaning Atherton was in charge and wouldn't come through the door first. Or so I hoped, because I wanted to turn him over to Clay and let my own beta get some answers. Then I'd return Atherton—alive—to Parker, and make damned sure every other Pack in the world knew what happened here. Parker might throw motherhood in my face, but there was nothing more precious to a Pack than its young. Prove Parker came after my kids and he'd find no sympathy anywhere.

So I waited. And continued to wait until I heard a whine from the office. Logan. Not a cry of pain but a question. *Mom? Where are you?*

I listened for any sound from the other side of the door, but at least five minutes had passed. How long did it take them to check a damn office?

Another whine, louder, worry seeping in. The scrabble of claws. I jogged down the hall to see Logan on his feet, Kate with her head up, blinking as she looked around.

Logan started my way, but his feet tangled like a newborn colt's and he went down. It would have been comical if it didn't prove they were in no shape to run. They were the equivalent of newborn wolves, unaccustomed to life on four legs.

I hurried over to them and ran my hand over Logan's head. He shook it off, then whined an apology, as if to say, *I appreciate the sentiment, Mom, but right now, I really just want to be up and walking.*

I crouched beside them and whispered. "Someone's found us. Two werewolves. They're in another office. I need you both—"

Kate leaped up, teeth flashing in a snarl, ears flattened. But like her brother, her body didn't work quite the way she expected. She lost her balance on the leap and toppled, muzzle first, to the floor and growled at it. Logan made a noise like a chuckle and nudged her, only to get a snap in return.

"Yes," I said. "You're in no shape to defend me. Or yourselves. So I need you to stay here and be quiet. I'm going to peek into the hall—"

Footsteps. Two pairs.

Logan nudged my hand. *We're fine, Mom. Go on.*

I crept back to the door. Through it, I could hear the footsteps better. Different footsteps this time, one pair lighter, clicking against the linoleum. Not boots or sneakers. Pumps. Women's shoes.

I eased the door open just enough to inhale and—

I pushed it wider and leaned out, whispering, "Here!"

Nick might have been the one with super-hearing, but it was Vanessa who turned first, her gun raised. Seeing me, she lowered it quickly and hurried over. I let them through and motioned them into the suite. I forgot what they'd see there until Kate started to growl, stifling it when she caught their scents.

Vanessa stopped. She was in the lead, and the first to see what—or who—lay on the floor.

"Oh, my God," she whispered. "They... Both..."

"Apparently," I said. "It's been a busy night."

Nick let out a low whistle and slipped past Vanessa. "Look at you two. I know you're quick studies, but this is just showing off. How old are you again? Seven?"

Kate exhaled a sigh and rolled her eyes.

"You're Logan, right?" Nick said to her.

Another sigh. Another eye-roll. Nick chuckled under his breath. They might not be much different in size, but if the fur color didn't give it away, the eye rolls would have. Nick crouched and reached out to rub Kate under the chin. She growled and yanked back. Apparently, a pat was fine, but a chin rub was just beneath her dignity. He chuckled again and scratched her around the neck.

"You look just like your dad at your age," he said. "This is going to be fun. We'll go for runs, and I'll chase you and knock you down and bully you, just like your dad did—"

She snapped at his hand. He pulled it back and looked at the fang dents.

"Or not." He turned to Logan. "So how about you? Surprised us all, huh? Playing stoic while your sister got everyone in a tizzy, drama queen that she is—"

Kate snapped at him again, teeth biting only air this time, a warning. He gave her a look. "If the collar fits…"

Logan nudged Nick's hand, allowing a single pat, before backing up and turning to me, expectantly. *There are still werewolves in the building, right?*

Vanessa interpreted the look before I did. She was still standing back, staring at the twins. When Logan glanced at her, she said, "They aren't ready to leave, are they." A statement, not a question, but Kate rose, bristling.

"Yes, Kate," Vanessa said. "I'm sure you feel fine, but you've just changed from a girl to a wolf. If we want to get out of here safely, the exit plan does not involve you running down stairs on four legs. Nick can barely do stairs after thirty years' experience."

"Hey," Nick said.

"It's true," Vanessa said.

Kate dipped her muzzle, acknowledging the point.

"Can I stay with them?" Vanessa asked me. "You and Nick are better equipped for handling the intruders."

When I hesitated, she lifted her gun, reminding me she was armed and, if I was being honest, perhaps in a better position to defend the kids against two men barreling through that door.

"Leave them in this room," I said. "You take the hall. Anyone except Pack comes through that door…"

"They're going down. Anyone you want alive?" She hesitated, glanced at the kids and then mouthed, *Sorry*, to me.

"If injuring them is enough, do that," I said. "The more hostages the better. They're definitely British Pack."

Malcolm? She mouthed the name, her back to the twins.

I nodded, which she knew meant, *If it's him, shoot to kill.* No messing around there.

"Can you do that?" I asked, and she knew I didn't mean whether she could defend the children or shoot the British wolves.

"Happily, as much as I know I shouldn't say that about any target."

"You have good reason."

Nick gave the kids a farewell pat and I said a few words to them, just, "Hang tight, rest up, love you." Then we were off. ⌒

Twenty-five

EFORE WE LEFT, we checked our cell phones again. When Vanessa had found Nick, he'd realized he couldn't get in touch with any of us. They'd gone to the hotel, discovered the empty room and followed our trail. Which meant that no one else knew our predicament.

Nick took the lead. Alpha might mean "first in Pack" but it never meant "first through a door." We reached what seemed like the right office suite, judging by where I'd heard the voices. I dropped, sniffed and found two trails—Atherton and his partner. Nick and I listened. Only one set, meaning they'd gone in and hadn't come out. That'd been close to fifteen minutes ago, and all was silent inside.

Nick mouthed, *Nap time?* with a smile. I rolled my eyes and straightened.

Two werewolves are hot on a trail. Both go into a room. Neither comes out. Any solution I could come up with sounded about as preposterous as Nick's joke.

"Trap?" I whispered.

Nick made a face, which told me it was as unlikely as I thought. I stepped back for a better and wider vantage point, ears pricked for any sounds from inside, eyes attuned for any shift of shadows, betraying movement. Nick slowly opened the door and stepped inside. I followed and eased it shut behind me. We stood there, inhaling and listening and peering into the dark office. I could smell the werewolves and...

I took a deep breath. The hair on my neck rose. I glanced at Nick. He frowned back. I bent, but didn't pick up the scent there. It seemed to come from the air, so faint I wasn't surprised Nick didn't detect it.

I mouthed a name, and Nick stiffened. Then he swung toward the door. I caught his forearm and shook my head.

The scent I picked up? Malcolm.

Vanessa and the kids were safe. To get to them from here, Malcolm would have to walk past us or climb out the window. Only Spider-Man could manage the window route from three floors up, and I'm reasonably sure that none of those Nast experiments involved giving him web-slinging powers.

I took in the layout of the office suite. It was the same design as the one we'd come from. I started forward. Nick laid his hand on my shoulder and mouthed, "Women at two paces." I shot him the finger but let him pass and then followed at his heels.

There was one door on our right. Nick peeked in. He inhaled and shook his head, but then motioned for a second opinion. I stuck my head into the dark room. No werewolf scent here at all. I dropped to one knee and checked the carpet. Spilled coffee, spilled curry, spilled semen. I looked up. Sex in the doorway? Whatever does it for you, I guess. Point was, no werewolves had passed through here.

Nick crept toward the main office. Then he stopped. His head tilted. I walked up behind him, and he fluttered his fingers. A half-hearted warning that said, "You're supposed to stay back," more than, "I will insist you stay back."

I looked past him. Moonlight shone through the windows, illuminating a quartet of desks—and two office workers, seated at theirs, one with his head forward on his keyboard, arms crossed as a pillow, the other slumped back in his chair. Both seemingly sound asleep. Burning the midnight oil so long they'd drifted off. Except I didn't even need to catch a whiff of scent to know these weren't office workers. And they weren't asleep.

It was the British wolves. Atherton and his flunky. Dead. Their bodies had been staged, but not to fool us into thinking they were sleepy office workers. No, staged as an amusing tableau. The guys who'd fallen asleep on the job. Werewolves who'd screwed up, been caught off guard, and sent to their eternal slumber in reward. Their killer had even put a pen behind Atherton's ear and wrapped the other guy's hand around a coffee cup.

"Malcolm," Nick muttered.

There was no sign of him, but as I moved in, I caught the faint whiff of his scent in the air. I crouched. No sign of it on the carpet. He'd taken precautions, then, with the scent suppressor as he'd snuck up and killed these two.

Why kill them? Because he could. As I'd reminded myself yesterday, Malcolm didn't have partners. He had lackeys. Even in the Pack it had been like that.

It was possible these two had turned on Malcolm, but more likely, they'd only outlived their usefulness. The British Alpha was probably second-guessing the wisdom of this mission as he realized I wasn't as clueless as he expected. He may have recalled his wolves. He may have just told them to be more cautious. Either way, Malcolm wouldn't tolerate the breach of his authority. The British wolves hadn't produced results and now they were causing him grief. So they'd died.

The moment I was certain Malcolm was no longer in that office, I was out the door. Nick and I ran back to where we'd left Vanessa and the kids. When the door at the far end of the hall opened, I had only to see the hand on the knob to know who it was.

I raced into the office, leaving Nick to tell the newcomer what was going on, but I don't think Nick even got a word out, because as soon as Clay saw me running, his footsteps thundered down the hall. He pushed Nick aside and found me standing just inside the office suite, facing a gun. He sprang before he realized who was holding that gun. Vanessa let out a yelp. Clay cursed and redirected his lunge. I ignored both of them and ran into the main office where the twins were curled up together, both heads raised sleepily.

"They're fine," I breathed. "Thank God."

I leaned on the nearest desk for support. Clay strode around the corner and stopped short as he stared at the two young wolves.

"Um…" he said.

"It's okay," I said. "They were like that when I left."

He turned to stare at me. I sputtered a laugh. Kate joined in with a snorting wheeze, and Logan gave a chuckling growl.

"Your kids," I said. "Or pups, apparently. They grow up fast, don't they?"

He continued to stare. The twins rose and made their way over. Kate bumped his hand. Logan sat on his haunches and snarled a yawn.

"They're fine," I said.

"I can see that."

He bent in front of Kate, one hand rubbing her neck as the other reached for Logan. I stepped back to give them a moment, but Clay caught my hand. His gaze met mine and he smiled, not a blazing grin but a slow, careful smile. Logan's smile. The one that said, tentatively: *This is good, right?*

I smiled back and squeezed his hand. "Everything's okay. A huge shock, but it's over, and they're just resting while I..."

My gaze shot to the door as I remembered what we'd been doing. At that moment, a door slapped shut somewhere.

"It's Malcolm," I said. "He ki— He's out there." I started for the door. "Stay with the kids. Nick?"

Clay got to his feet, hand grabbing me. When I looked at him, he murmured, "I'd rather..." That was all he needed to say. I nodded. If I was going after Malcolm, Clay wanted to be with me. The kids were fine—to get to them, Malcolm would need to get through us.

We stepped into the hall. And our target stood right there, midway between the stairwell door and ours. Only it wasn't Malcolm. It was Parker's cousin, Harris. The guy who'd approached me in London to talk about Atherton.

When Harris saw us, he ran.

"Predictable," Clay muttered.

"Too."

"Window or stairs?" he asked as we jogged down the hall.

"Stairs."

He swore.

I grinned and said, "Being Alpha has its advantages. Enjoy."

Clay spun. He kicked open the door beside us. As I raced into the stairwell, I heard the muffled crash of breaking glass.

Harris missed the sound. Or didn't know what it portended. He kept going, shoes clattering down the steps. He didn't even glance back to see who was in pursuit. Idiot. Also somewhat disappointing, because if he had, I'm sure he would have decided I was the lesser threat and circled back, and I was kind of hoping for the chance to beat the shit out of at least one of the guys who'd come after my kids.

He clambered down to the first floor and shot out the stairwell door without even a backward glance. I followed. Harris veered around the corner down the side hall to the back door. I reached the end just as he threw it open...and saw Clay standing there.

"Hello," Clay said.

Harris wheeled and ran at me. I waited. He kept coming. I don't know what he expected, but a pile drive to the gut didn't seem to be it. He staggered back, gasping. Clay grabbed him by the collar.

"In here," I said, backing into the corridor. While there was no guarantee Malcolm wasn't already in the building, I'd rather take care of this guy where we could see both exits. As Clay hauled Harris to me, I texted Nick. *On first floor. Occupied. Double-watch, pls.*

He texted back in a second. *Already triple. Quadruple now.*

I smiled and sent a quick, *Thx.*

Clay had Harris in front of me now, holding him up on his tiptoes.

"You don't want to kill me," Harris said.

"Mmm, yeah," Clay said. "Kinda do."

"I have information."

"Good for you." Clay leaned forward to look around at his face. "But you know what's better than information? Setting an example. Telling others what happens to anyone who comes after my kids."

Harris's expression suggested the infamous photos of Clay "setting an example" thirty years ago had made their way across the pond. Or stories of them, anyway, which were always worse, as the years passed and legend grew, and it'd been a damned ugly one to begin with.

"I-it wasn't me," Harris said. "And no one was going to hurt your children. That wasn't the plan."

He waited for us to ask what the plan had been. Instead, Clay looked at me. We made eye contact. No words exchanged. He loosened his grip on Harris. The British wolf wrenched free and dove past me. I let him. Clay let him, too, just standing there, watching. I counted to two. Then I tore after him. I dove at his back, grabbed his shirt and took him down. He twisted and swung. I blocked. Then it was my turn.

I beat the shit out of Harris Charles Parker. I did not escape unscathed, of course. I'm a very good fighter; I'm not a perfect one. I'd have a half-dozen bruises and possibly a black eye. By the time I finished, Harris could barely speak, his face swollen, battered beyond recognition as he huddled on the floor, coughing blood.

"You're as crazy as he is," he coughed, gasping as he peered at me through the one eye that still opened.

Clay snorted. "That was nothing. Imagine what you'd have gotten if she thought you really *had* been trying to hurt our kids."

"So you—you did that—"

"—for *going after* them," I said. "If you'd touched them, you wouldn't be talking. You'd be alive, though. And wishing otherwise."

He cursed us both for that, hurling every insult he could dream up. Clay lifted him by the back of the collar and hauled him to his feet, facing me again. He had to hold Harris upright to keep him there. One leg was twisted at a bad angle, and he kept coughing, speckling the walls with blood.

I reached into his pocket. He was wearing a light jacket, unnecessary in August, even at night, but when I'd been battering him, I'd realized he had something stuffed in one pocket. I pulled out a shirt. It was in a plastic bag that hadn't quite contained the scent of the man who'd worn it.

When I removed the shirt, the scent burst forth, as strong as if the man himself had been standing beside us.

"Malcolm, I presume," I said.

Harris managed to snort. "I thought you'd have that particular smell ingrained—"

"No," I cut him off and waggled the shirt. "I mean *this* is Malcolm. This is what we smelled. The man himself is still in Bulgaria."

Behind Harris, Clay's eyes widened. Then, after barely a two-second pause, he mouthed *Fuck*, as he put the pieces together. We'd smelled Malcolm only a few times, mostly as a distant scent, and never on the ground. We'd texted with him, but anyone who knew Malcolm—or his reputation—could pull off that conversation. They'd also know to stage the two dead bodies to look like his work.

Harris sneered. "Did you really think we'd work with that psychopath? Hollis is right. You Americans aren't too bright. Wave a shirt around, and you start chasing your tails, searching for your bogeyman."

"Maybe," I said. "But we still caught you, didn't we?" I gestured for Clay to bring him upstairs where I could question him properly. ⌒

Twenty-six

WE INTERROGATED HARRIS in the office beside the one where Nick waited with the kids. Which meant, yes, more destruction to private property. We weren't concerned. There were no security cameras and even if we left blood, it wasn't ours and no one was going to be analyzing it to discover the identity of vandals. The bodies down the hall would be long gone by the time anyone came to work tomorrow morning.

We'd barely gotten Harris upstairs when Jeremy and Reese arrived, Madison having finally gotten through. Quick explanation—our kids are wolves and Malcolm's in Bulgaria—and while they figured out that, I sent Nick and Reese to find the others and have them scour the area for any remaining Brits. Jeremy and Noah would be on "crime-scene duty," making sure we'd left nothing behind with the bodies here or at the hotel. Vanessa stayed. As much as I loved my wolves, I kind of liked having my kids protected by someone with a gun.

Next we questioned Harris. Or I did, while Clay made sure he answered. The latter didn't take much—Harris was beaten badly enough that a little pressure applied on the right spot was enough to have him howling...behind the sock stuffed into his mouth, of course, so we didn't distress our children with the sounds of torture. Family comes first.

Harris talked. According to him, this was step one in Parker's plan to take over the American Pack. Get a couple of shirts from a Bulgarian wolf who had contact with Malcolm. Bring me to England on the pretense of arranging Parker's son's stay in the U.S. Tap my phone and e-mails to find out where Clay had the kids. Send the fake messages and have someone follow me around London, putting me on edge. Then, when I return to the U.S., jump into action.

The beta and his team had left London twelve hours before I did, and had been in place at the cabin. They'd planned to lure Logan away the next morning. Kate coming outside had been a fortuitous opportunity that they'd taken full advantage of. Then they'd played us, seeding the forest with Malcolm's scent, and having a couple wolves terrorize Logan and Reese in the cabin. They denied having sent the texts, but that was bullshit. There had been, as Harris said earlier, no intention to hurt the children. In fact, that would run counter to their plan, which was to show exactly how inept and hapless the American Pack had become, run by a hysterical mother who flipped out at even the suggestion of harm to her darling children.

I listened, and I believed about twenty-five percent of it. For one thing, it was an awful lot of work just to make fools of us. Two, it didn't explain why Harris had cornered me in London to discuss the British Alpha. Three? Those bodies in the office.

"What bodies?" Harris said.

"Atherton and one of your companions." I described the other guy, but as soon as I said Atherton's name, Harris seemed to stop listening, going pale and then saying, "Like bloody hell. You murdered them and—"

"And staged them to look like sleeping office workers? A classic Malcolm prank? To what purpose?"

"So you could blame Malcolm, because you still thought he was in on it."

"Mutts blame others for kills," I said. "Pack doesn't. We take a life, we take responsibility. If your beta came after us on our territory, we had every right to kill him. That's international law. If you didn't kill him, then I'd suggest you have a mutiny on your hands. Whoever else you brought over didn't like the way things were going."

With that, Harris started to curse. I left him there with Clay and went back into the other office to make a long-distance call.

"I have your cousin here," I said to Parker. "And your beta is about a hundred feet away. Would you like to tell me again that none of your wolves are on my territory? Or would you rather wait until I start sending body parts?"

Silence on the other end of the line. Then Parker said, "You can send me their heads if you like. And not as proof they were there."

"Are you sure? Turning your back on your wolves after you sent them on a covert mission? How will the rest of your Pack feel about that?"

More silence. Then, "Covert mission?"

"To embarrass me, of course. Hopefully enough to turn my allies against my Pack and help you recover a little of your former empire. That is what you were doing, right? I've got Harris in the next room and he swears—"

That's when Parker himself started swearing. And declaring decapitation was too good for Harris and the others. He wanted them back, alive, so he could deal with them...and he'd send me pictures of their heads. On spikes.

As I'd surmised by this point, Parker's only crime was being an arrogant son of a bitch who never would admit he'd lost control of his Pack and that four wolves—including his beta—had gone AWOL. Apparently, he'd already dispatched another four to retrieve them, hopefully before they did anything stupid and pulled him into a war with the American Pack.

That, it seemed, had been Atherton's real purpose. To embarrass his Alpha and turn Parker's supporters in the British Pack against him. To give Atherton another shot at Alpha-hood. Harris had tried to lay the groundwork for this in his conversation with Nick that night in London. The irony is that Nick and I never discussed that meeting. We would have, eventually, but it wasn't worth dealing with before my vacation. Which meant even if they *had* succeeded, I'd never have jumped to the conclusion they wanted—that Parker was an inept leader, unsupported by his Pack, ripe for mutiny.

In the end, to add more irony, Parker was indeed embarrassed. He had to admit to internal dissent, which left him in no position to bully me. With his Pack ripped in half, he was in need of a little support himself, which I was more than happy to give, generous soul that I am. In return, he'd bring his allies on board in our dispute against the Australians and, perhaps more personally satisfying, I got to hear the words, "I was wrong about you," leave his mouth. Whether he meant it didn't matter, because I *knew* he was wrong about me. I might not have defeated the worst threat my Pack faced, but I'd solved the most immediate one. And I'd done it while dealing with my eight-year-old twins unexpectedly transforming into wolves. Not bad. Not bad at all. ⌒

Twenty-seven

$\mathcal{I}$ DID NOT TAKE Parker at his word when he disavowed knowledge of his beta's treachery. True, I suspect no Alpha would lie about that. Mutiny is a more crushing admission than claiming you tried to overthrow another Pack. And I'd like to think no Alpha would turn on his own wolves like that. Still, I wanted proof. We found the remaining Brit and took him and Harris back to Stonehaven, where they spent a day in the cage being "convinced" to tell the truth while our kids enjoyed a holiday at the Sorrentino estate. The Brits cracked on day two and admitted to exactly what Parker claimed. With that, I had Karl and Antonio escort them to England for Parker to deal with.

After they left, Clay and I had twelve hours to kill before the kids returned with Jeremy. We spent it in bed. It'd been a long and difficult weekend. We needed a rest. Or something like that.

I was indeed sleeping when the phone rang. Dreaming of being trapped in a pizza factory, which might have had something to do with the fact that the bed was littered with pizza crusts and smeared with sauce, the remains of a couple of frozen ones we'd dug up earlier.

I escaped the pizza factory and lifted my head to hear Clay say, "If Jeremy's calling to say he's coming back early, tell him not to rush."

"Why? You need more sleep?"

"Nope." He rolled over, hand sliding to my rear, flipping me onto my back.

"Um, phone?" I said as it continued to ring.

"Yep, that's what it is." He slid on top of me. "Better yet, tell him to spend another night there. I want to run. Hunt. Spend the night out. Just you and me. We haven't done that in years."

"I agree. However, in order to answer the phone, I need to be able to reach it."

I lifted my arm, and waggled it. He pinned my wrist over my head and pushed into me.

I gasped. "Okay, definitely not answering now."

"He'll wait." He took my other wrist, stretching it over my head as he pushed in all the way, making me gasp. The phone stopped ringing. His lips went to my ear. "No rush to answer. The kids are fine now. Everything's fine."

"It is, isn't it?"

"It really is."

We meant more than the danger we'd overcome. Our kids had Changed and they were full werewolves, and they were fine, and years of stress and worry were gone now.

I arched back against the pillow. "I want to go with you next month. To Austin. For your lectures?"

He looked down at me. "Yeah?"

"Yeah. Been a while since we did that, too."

"It has."

"The kids are okay."

"They are."

"And we could use the break."

"We could."

"More breaks in general. Now that they're getting older."

"Hell, yeah."

He pushed in again and I tugged my hands from his grasp to pull him into a kiss, fingers entwined in his hair, hips rising to meet his.

"Hell, yeah," I murmured, and he laughed.

❧

WE'D BARELY FINISHED when the phone rang again. Clay groaned.

"Hey, he waited ten minutes," I said. "He knows his timing."

A low laugh as Clay reached over me for the phone.

"Remember," he said as he held it out to me. "Tell him to make it an overnight trip."

"Why don't you tell him that yourself?"

"I'm not Alpha."

I laughed, kissed his shoulder and answered the phone with, "Hey."

"Hey, yourself," said a voice that was not Jeremy's. "You're in a good mood. Pleased with your success? Or enjoying a little private time with Clayton while the kids are away?"

I scrambled upright. "Where—?"

"Oh, you recognize my voice. Excellent. Don't worry, Elena. Your children are perfectly safe from me. I have my faults. Hurting children is not among them. Particularly not such fascinating little ones. Did I hear correctly? That they've had their first Change already?"

Clay grabbed the phone. Before I could protest, he had it on speaker, held between us.

"Malcolm," he said.

"Ah, Clayton. Taking the phone from your mate before she flies into a panic?"

"No," I said. "I'm still here."

"Both of you? That's so sweet. You make an excellent team, you know. As co-Alphas."

"I'm not—" Clay began.

"Yes, yes. I know the story, and I think it's very modern of you, Clayton, letting your wife pretend to be in charge. Keeps the home life happy, I suppose. And that's what I want to talk about. Home." A two-second pause. "I want to come back."

I choked on a laugh. Clay managed a strangled curse.

"That doesn't sound very welcoming," Malcolm said.

"Oh, we'll be plenty welcoming," I said. "Why don't you come to Stonehaven right now. We'd love to see you again. If you can make it in the next few hours, it would be a wonderful surprise for Jeremy when he gets home. Your corpse. With a bow."

"I see why you two are so happy together. Equally ruthless. You've trained her well, Clayton. I'll admit I'm a little offended. After all, I did give you two a gift, though admittedly, I forgot the bow. I know you got my present. Two very sleepy office workers..."

My gut went cold.

"Shall I provide details, so you can be sure it was me?" He did. And they matched exactly.

Malcolm went on. "I caught wind of the Brits' little scheme. Well, after I tortured the Bulgarian cur who stole my shirts. I liked those ones. He found out what the Brits had planned, so I let him live. Though he may have regretted that, after I was done. I used their own tricks for covering my scent as best I could. I delivered little Kate's shoe to Elena. I sent the texts to warn you about Logan. And I killed those two who were hurting you. My gift. To protect your children."

When we said nothing, he cleared his throat. "That doesn't sound like thank you."

"It's not," Clay said. "But as Elena said, you're welcome to come here and get our appreciation in person."

Malcolm only chuckled. "No, that's quite all right. I don't expect appreciation. It was a gesture of good faith. A demonstration of my usefulness. I said I'm no threat to your little ones, and I'm not. In fact, I could be the best friend two doting werewolf parents ever had. I want to come home. Not to Stonehaven. I know you'd never allow that. Give me territory and give me protection. And, of course, give me supervision. Impose any rules and restrictions on me, and I will follow them. To the letter. I will be absolutely no threat to anyone in your—*our*—Pack. But to your enemies?" Another chuckle. "That's quite another story."

"I would never do that to—" I stopped myself before I said I'd never do that to Jeremy. He certainly wouldn't want me saying so to Malcolm. Even as I thought it, I realized this was something we'd need to discuss, that Clay and I couldn't make the choice again to keep Jeremy out of it. When we told him

Malcolm's proposition, though, I feared his reply wouldn't be the cut-and-dry "Hell, no" I wanted.

"Don't answer now. Take a few days. Think about it. Think long and hard about it." For the first time since we'd begun speaking, all traces of mocking humor left his voice. "I'm tired of running. I'm tired of needing to run. Not just from you. I have enemies, as you might imagine, and you are, to be honest, among the least of them. You want me dead, but you do not wish to risk anyone in your Pack when I'm not an immediate threat. You're smart and you're cunning and you're loyal. Both of you, and that is no sop to your pride, Elena. You aren't Clayton's equal, but I accept you as his partner. I respect your ability to lead a Pack far more than I do your predecessor. The two of you will discuss this, and you will come up with a plan that will allow my safe return to the Pack, because you know I'm better there, under your watch, than I am in the wild."

I looked at Clay. He rubbed his mouth, shaking his head, and I knew the answer wasn't yes—I couldn't imagine it being yes—but nor was it an automatic no. We needed to think. To talk and to think.

Malcolm continued. "I will accept a dozen transmitters, Elena. I will allow round-the-clock surveillance. I will take whatever is needed to convince you that I can, in my way, be trusted. At least in my loyalty to the Pack. No one has ever questioned that. Right to the end, I was loyal and I never laid a finger on anyone in it. Not even my son. I'm tired of the games. That's all they are. Games."

"You tried to kill Nick—"

"I *told* his girlfriend I'd kill him to avenge myself on his father for betraying me during the ascension fight. Did I mean it? Of course not. Nicky fought well—his father and Clayton have finally taught him something. But if I wanted to kill him, I could have found another way. He's an easy target. Too trusting by far. It was a game."

"And Vanessa?"

"Is that his girlfriend? Yes, I would have killed her. Without question. She isn't Pack, and it would have taught Nicky a lesson about coming after me. But now, presuming you'd be upset if I hurt her, she—and the other women—will be, as far as I'm concerned, mates of my Pack brothers, off limits in every way. You set the rules. I follow them. I keep my word. If I refuse to agree to your conditions, then we are no worse off than we are now, chasing one another like the Road Runner and Wile E. Coyote. Amusing, but ultimately futile and frustrating."

Clay lifted his hand, fingers spread.

"Five days," I said. "In the meantime, get the hell off our territory. I don't care where you go, but I want a call from you in the next twelve hours from the other side of an ocean, and I will have the top technicians at my disposal check to be sure it's a legitimate long-distance call. Then you will telephone, from the same region, every four hours until we meet—by coming to see you."

"Understood. I will speak to you in less than twelve hours. At this number?"

"No." I gave him my cell. "If you contact anyone in the Pack other than myself or Clay, the answer is no."

"Understood and agreed. You'll hear from me soon."

He hung up. I looked at Clay.

"Shit," I said.

"Yeah." He pushed up from the bed. "You want a drink?"

"Please…or, maybe, just bring the bottle."

He nodded and headed from the room as I fell back on the bed and stared at the ceiling. It was going to be a long night. ⌒